DEADLY VINES
A WITCH IN THE WOODS

JENNA ST. JAMES

Deadly Vines

Jenna St. James

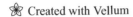 Created with Vellum

"I still think this is ridiculous," GiGi grumbled. "And I'm talking about both the license *and* this car!"

GiGi and I were currently cruising the back roads of Enchanted Island in the Princess Lolly—a two-person vehicle made to look like something the Candyland princess would drive. It was cotton candy pink with yellow and orange lollipops welded onto the roof. While incredibly tiny, it *was* street legal and topped out at fifty miles per hour. It had no AC, heat, or radio…but it was the perfect vehicle for GiGi to learn to drive in, no matter what she said.

I smiled and looked out the passenger-side window so she wouldn't catch me laughing. "You know why you need to have a license, GiGi. With all the changes coming soon, you need to have a way to get around on the island other than on your Vespa."

"Been doing it for years," GiGi pouted. "Don't see why it has to change now."

Two weeks ago, when my gargoyle boyfriend, Alex

Stone, asked me to marry him on Valentine's Day, he unknowingly put into play a lot of other changes. Now Mom was building a small cottage on the land between my castle and Black Forest where my dad lived...GiGi was giving her cottage to my cousin Serena and her werewolf husband, Detective Grant Wolfe...and GiGi was moving into Mom's house in town.

But in order for GiGi to move to town, she needed a valid driver's license so she could get around—something she'd never had.

"I blame Alex Stone for this nonsense," GiGi said.

"He's just trying to keep you legal and prepare for the unknown."

"Speaking of the unknown," GiGi said, "how're you coming on that thing you're tracking?"

During an investigation two weeks back, I stumbled across some interesting drag marks down by the water on the south side of the island. I'd been trying to track the animal that had made the marks during my downtime as the game warden for Enchanted Island. Unfortunately, I wasn't having much luck, other than discovering some disturbing half-eaten carcasses along the south shores.

"I think it's staying mostly on the south side of the island." I grabbed hold of the dashboard. "You're coming up to a turn. You need to slow down."

"I am."

"Slow down, GiGi!" When she didn't slow down, I slammed my foot on the floorboard, thinking that might help.

It didn't.

"Dammit! Slow down!" With my left hand still on the dash, I grabbed the safety bar above the window and held on tight. "Slow down!"

GiGi finally applied the brakes—causing us to fishtail as she took the corner on two wheels.

"Stop! Stop the car!" I turned and glared at her. "I mean it! I'm done. I want out! I'll call Alex and have him fly here and get me. I'm done riding with you. You're insane!"

"Oh, hush. It's these brakes. I'm not used to them, is all. Besides, I warded this ridiculous vehicle. If we roll or flip, it'll be like rolling on fluffy clouds."

I rolled my eyes, but didn't argue. Thanks to GiGi warding my Bronco, she'd saved my life *and* Needles' life on two separate occasions. I counted to ten and once again reminded myself it could be worse—I could have Needles in the car.

Needles was my bodyguard, of sorts. My dad, Black Forest King, insisted I take him with me everywhere I went for protection. It didn't matter I was about to turn forty-one and had been in some type of law enforcement job for over twenty years. Dad still wanted the flying and talking porcupine to watch over me.

Today, Needles had elected to stay back at the castle and catch up on his sleep. He wasn't a fool—he wanted nothing to do with GiGi and learning to drive.

"Where are we going, anyway?" I asked.

"Just out for a leisurely Sunday mid-afternoon drive."

I snorted. "There's nothing leisurely about this drive."

"Very funny. Selma called me last night. She wants me to stop by."

Selma Craftsman had been GiGi's best friend for well over eighty years. The two ornery witches may not see a lot of each other anymore except at coven meetings, but they spoke over the phone on a weekly basis.

"Did she say why?" I asked.

"Nope. But I heard worry in her voice."

GiGi made a right, and we bumped along slowly down a

rutted path between the trees. Most of Enchanted Island was covered in plants, trees, shrubs, and vegetation. Trees and plants you wouldn't expect to find growing together were commonplace here. As more and more people settled on the island, more construction and building had become a necessity—except for the north side. My father refused to let anyone but me and my immediate family roam that area of the island. Every citizen on Enchanted Island knew and agreed not to cross my father on that one rule...or suffer the consequences.

"Good thing the Lolly is so small," I said. "We'd never get through here in my Bronco."

As we neared Selma's place, the path got narrower and narrower. When the tree branches scraped against our windows, GiGi finally stopped.

"We'll need to walk from here," GiGi said. "It's not too far, maybe fifty yards. I think I see smoke rising from Selma's fireplace."

I zipped up my jacket as we exited the Lolly and walked toward the smoke. Even though we were about to cross into March, it was still a little cool with the breeze coming off the Atlantic ocean.

Glancing around, my footsteps faltered. Something wasn't right. There were no birds chirping or animals running through the woods, and the trees were giving off a weird vibe.

I stopped next to a redwood and laid my palm against its trunk. I was about to communicate with the tree—a trait I'd inherited from my dad—when GiGi interrupted me.

"What's wrong?" GiGi demanded.

"I don't know. Something's not right. Can't you feel it in the air? No birds, nothing scampering about. Plus, I'm getting a weird vibe from the trees. Hold on and let me see what's going on."

I closed my eyes and formed a connection with the old redwood. *"Hello, friend. I'm headed to see Selma, the witch in the cottage. Is there danger about?"*

"Something strange. Something not natural."

I was about to ask what he meant when an ear-piercing scream reverberated through the trees.

"Selma!" GiGi cried, taking off toward the cottage as fast as her geriatric legs could carry her.

Cursing, I dropped my hand from the ancient tree and took off after GiGi.

2

"**W**ait!" I cried, grabbing GiGi by the arm when we were still a good distance away from the cottage. "We don't know what's going on, and I don't have my service weapon on me."

"She's obviously hurt," GiGi snapped. "Now, let go of me. We got magic. We'll be fine. I need to see about Selma."

We continued running until we reached the cottage.

"Let me go in first." I gently pushed GiGi aside and twisted the knob on the front door.

It opened effortlessly.

I stepped inside the dimly lit cottage and did a quick survey of the area. Nothing seemed out of place.

"Selma?" GiGi called out next to me. "Maybe she's in the kitchen."

I followed GiGi toward the back of the house, all the while straining to hear something—anything. But the house was deathly silent. Which made it even more heart-wrenching as

GiGi's anguished cry filled the air. Stepping around her, I glanced at the table at what was left of Selma Craftsman.

"By the goddess," GiGi whispered. "What's happened?"

I scanned the room, searching for whatever had done the horrific damage to Selma. The back door that led outside was wide open, but I didn't sense anyone else around. I tiptoed past the still-steaming mug of hot tea and the plate of cut fruit on the table and stopped next to the body. Reaching out, I tried to feel for a pulse—but seeing as how half her face and neck were gone, it was hard to do.

"What did this?" GiGi demanded, her voice now filled with rage.

I glanced down at the floor and sucked in a breath. "Stand back! Don't come any closer. I know these tracks."

I bent down and barely touched the top layer of goo on the hardwood floor. I knew what to expect from the touch—pain. Two of my fingertips *still* tingled from the first time I'd touched the goo without gloves nearly two weeks ago. I'd taken a sample into Finn Faeton, our forensics expert, and she told me the slime was acid based, which explained the searing pain I'd experienced.

"It's the same slimy substance I've seen all over the south side of the island." I stood and reached for my cell phone. "You okay, GiGi?"

GiGi shook her head, tears running down her wrinkled face as she sobbed quietly. "Why would someone do this to Selma? She was a sweet old witch who never hurt a soul."

My first instinct had been to run out the back door to see if I could find where the person or *thing* had gone, but I didn't want to leave GiGi alone. It was too much of a risk. GiGi may brag about having powerful magic, but Selma had powerful magic as well…and it hadn't helped her.

"I'll find out, GiGi," I said, pulling up Alex's contact number. "Promise."

Alex answered on the second ring. "Did you survive your ride with GiGi?"

I smiled. "I did. But we have a problem. We stopped by Selma Craftsman's cottage, and we found her dead." I turned my back on GiGi so she wouldn't overhear. "And it's bad, Alex. Her face looks like it's been half-eaten, and I found the same gooey substance on the floor that I've found at other sites recently."

Alex swore. "I'll call Doc Drago and Finn. So no need for an ambulance?"

"No. But it's a small hike to the cottage. You'll see where we parked the Lolly."

"I'll be there as fast as I can."

I gave him the address, then disconnected and slid the phone back inside the pocket of my yoga pants. "Why don't you go wait in the living room? Doc, Finn, and Alex should be here shortly."

Once GiGi ambled back to the front of the cottage, I used my magic to conjure an evidence bag. Whispering a levitation spell, I carefully moved the goo inside the baggie before placing it on the counter. Deciding to wait for the rest of the team, I went to be with GiGi.

"I hope this doesn't trigger Doc," GiGi sniffed, wiping the tears from her cheeks as she looked out Selma's window into the front yard.

Doc Drago had recently been thrusted into his own murderous nightmare. Not only was the woman he'd been casually seeing murdered, but it had all centered on the death of his first wife.

"Doc is strong." I gathered her up in my arms. "Right now, I just want to make sure *you're* okay."

GiGi laid her curly gray head against my chest. My diminutive grandma, usually so spunky and full of life, seemed like a scared little girl as she pressed her body into mine. "Selma was my best friend since grade school. It's like a piece of me is gone forever. Like when your grandpa died."

I blinked back my own tears at the mention of my grandpa. Swallowing past the lump in my throat, I patted GiGi's head. "We'll figure this out. I promise."

"Selma didn't have any kids, and her husband died years ago. Only family she has left on the island is a great-niece who comes and checks on her once a week."

"I'll get all that information from you once we get the scene processed and Doc takes the body."

GiGi nodded, then stepped back. "You think whatever did that to her is the same thing you've been tracking for a couple weeks now?"

"I do. I just don't understand why he or *it* came here. Why Selma?"

I saw Alex land in the front yard, wings outstretched from his stone body. My gargoyle fiancé met my eyes and smiled as he shifted back to human form and stepped inside the cabin.

"GiGi," he said. "I'm sorry for your loss."

"Thank you," she murmured.

I motioned him back to the kitchen.

"What did this?" he asked.

"Like I said, I found the same slimy substance on the floor that I've found the last two weeks on the island."

"Do you know if it's human or…"

I shrugged. "I don't know. And I feel so helpless and useless. I mean, how hard can it be to track this thing down?"

"Don't beat yourself up. I don't know for sure because the island is always changing, but there has to be at least sixty to ninety miles of coast on the south side of the island. That's a lot of terrain to cover." He gave me a one-armed hug. "We *will* find it. Now that this has happened, I have a reason to help you."

I sighed. "Whatever it is, it has moved from feasting on animals to feasting on humans."

"But why now?" Alex asked.

It was the same question I'd asked myself a dozen times since discovering Selma's body.

3

"This is bad." Finn Faeton stood, her multi-colored hair and vibrant-colored tattoos shining under the overhead light fixture. She was a diminutive sprite who stood no taller than five feet. "I've never seen anything like this before. It's weird. There are no discernible teeth marks anywhere on her face and neck, yet it looks like she's been half eaten."

"Could the gooey acid have done this to her?" I asked, pointing to the green slime on the side of Selma's face and neck.

"Maybe," Finn said. "It's too soon to tell."

"Whatever it is," I said, "it acts quickly. GiGi and I heard her scream, and from that time to the time it took to discover her, maybe three minutes had passed. And that's a big maybe."

"Hopefully, I'll have something more when I get her on my table," Doc said. "Such a tragedy. Selma was a good woman. She sometimes volunteered at the hospital. Did you know that? She was one of the witches who made salves and other soothing potions in the burn unit."

I nodded. "She volunteered at a couple different places on the island from what I understand."

Alex strode into the kitchen from the front room. "I've talked GiGi into letting your mom take her home. I told her you'd drive the Lolly back to her cottage later."

I groaned inwardly. I absolutely *hated* driving that silly car, but I wasn't going to argue about it now. I'd suck it up and drive the Lolly home if it meant GiGi would be with Mom.

"Got something!" Finn called out from the kitchen's back door. She held up something green in a pair of tiny tweezers. "Looks like it's plant based. Maybe a vine or something like that."

"Good eye, Finn," Alex said.

I sighed. "Maybe this will finally be the clue I've needed. I'm tired of guessing what this thing is."

Alex drew me away from the body. "I suppose you won't have a problem with us working together?"

I snorted. "Heck, no. I'd appreciate the help. You know I've been tracking this thing for two weeks now. It's personal." I held up my hand. "And don't even try to tell me not to make it personal—save your breath. This *thing* went and killed GiGi's best friend since childhood. It's personal."

"Understood," Alex said. "GiGi told me Selma's next-of-kin was her great-niece." Alex looked down at his notebook. "Belinda Seaton. Married a selkie and lives on the northwest side of the island."

"Sounds right. Are we doing the notification?"

"Yes. I thought you'd want to, seeing as how it's a family friend."

I nodded. "I think that would be best."

"Good. I'll fly us to my house, pick up the Blazer, and head from there."

"If I can have some help carrying the body out," Doc said, "you two could go on. Finn is almost done here, and since we rode together, she can help me unload the body when we get to the labs."

"Sure can," Finn said. "And I just need about five more minutes, then I'll be ready."

"I don't have anything to do tonight," Doc said. "I think I'll start on the autopsy when we return to the lab."

The forensic laboratories had recently undergone a remodel, thanks to a magic fight I'd gotten into with a vicious killer. But the major damage had been done when Doc's massive dragon form had torn through the walls as he was dragged outside the building.

"I can run the two samples I have as well," Finn said. "Jordan's working late tonight at his office, so I'm cool to stay and work."

"I'll make it up to you over drinks," I promised. "Girls' night soon."

Finn grinned. "Deal."

"What about Needles?" Alex asked. "You won't get home until late tonight. He's going to be upset he missed all the excitement."

I rolled my eyes. "I'll make it up to him by giving him a bag of pretzels before bedtime."

* * *

Tomlin and Belinda Seaton lived in a ranch-style shanty just twenty feet from the water. The seafoam green exterior blended in with the other vividly colored houses along the winding road.

"Last time we were in this neighborhood," Alex said as we exited his vehicle, "you were shot on the dock."

I winced. "I remember."

I walked up the two steps and knocked on Belinda's door. A few seconds later, it opened, and a curly-haired boy of about seven gave me a piercing look and narrowed his eyes. "Who are you?"

"I'm Shayla Loci, and this is Sheriff Stone."

"Yeah?" the boy mused. "Well, if you're the sheriff, then why don't you have on your uniform?"

Alex smiled. "I was off duty when I got a call."

"Huh." The boy put his hands on his hips. "You probably should have put on your uniform before you left the house. That's probably in the rules somewhere."

I bit my lip to keep from laughing. "Is your mom home?"

"Yeah." He turned and yelled into the house. "Mom! It's the cops!"

"What did you say?" Belinda strolled into the living room, wiping her hands on a dishrag. When she saw us, her smile froze, and I saw worry in her eyes. "What's wrong? Is it Tomlin?"

"No, ma'am," Alex said. "Could we come in?"

"Yes, of course. I'm sorry. I was in the middle of cooking dinner. Tomlin should be docking soon from fishing." She motioned us inside. "Kevin, go on in the kitchen and help your sister set the table."

"Aww, Mom! That's so lame. I wanna hear what the sheriff has to say."

"Do as I said," Belinda said sharply, worry making her statement come out harsher than I'm sure she meant. "Please, Kevin."

He shrugged. "Sure."

Once he was gone, Belinda rounded on me. "I know you. Your grandma and Aunt Selma are friends. Is this about Selma?"

I nodded. "I'm afraid it is, Belinda." I took a deep breath. "I'm sorry to tell you that Selma was attacked in her cottage today and killed."

Belinda let out a ragged cry and grabbed onto the stair's newel post. "What? You're sure? How? Who did this? Was she—what? This just doesn't make sense."

"Mom?" a little girl's voice came from another room. "Is everything okay?"

Belinda straightened and drew in a breath. "Yes, honey. Everything's fine. Stay in the kitchen, please." She looked back at me. "You're sure?"

I nodded. "Positive. I'm sorry, Belinda. GiGi and I drove out to see Selma around four-thirty and found her."

"You said she was attacked? It wasn't a heart attack or something like that?"

I glanced at Alex before answering. "It's too soon to say the exact cause of death, but it wasn't natural."

Belinda closed her eyes. "Who would want to hurt Aunt Selma? She was a sweet old witch. Kept to herself a lot, but always made the coven meetings and volunteered whenever she could. As far as I knew, everyone loved her."

Alex cleared his throat. "So you can't think of anyone who'd want to hurt her?"

"Mercy, no. Like I said, she was just a kind old woman. She was all alone now that my uncle passed, so I always made it a point to stop by at least once a week."

"And the last time you spoke with her?" Alex asked.

Belinda pursed her lips and looked up at the ceiling. "I'd say Friday night. I ran out to her cottage after work and stayed for about thirty minutes."

"Everything was fine?" I asked. "She didn't say anything about anyone watching her? Or maybe threatening her?"

"No. Nothing like that. We just talked about our week. I asked her if she needed anything from the grocery store, and then I left." Belinda pressed her lips together as a sob escaped. "Sorry. I just can't believe this is happening." She shook her head. "I can't believe someone would want to hurt Aunt Selma." She gasped and turned to me. "Wait. I just thought of something. I remember a couple weeks ago Aunt Selma telling me about a letter she got from Isaac Flowerbaum. He was angry with her because she had started a petition to stop the construction of a new bar outside town. It wasn't so much the bar she objected to, but the fact it was near a stream where local animals frequented. Anyway, Isaac told her she better stop making waves if she knew what was good for her. I saw the letter on her desk in the living room."

I knew Isaac Flowerbaum. Or rather, I knew *of* Isaac Flowerbaum. There were only two major construction companies on the island—Flowerbaum Construction and Stryker Construction.

"Thanks, Belinda," I said. "We'll start there."

We stepped outside into the chilly night air and strolled over to the Blazer.

"You want to talk to Isaac tonight or in the morning?" I asked.

"Morning. I want to find out more about this bar first." He started the Bronco and pulled out of the driveway. "What kind of supernatural is Isaac Flowerbaum? Witch or Fairy?"

"Woodland fairy."

4

Ten minutes later, as we crossed into the town limits, my cell phone rang.

"Hey, Mom. What's up? How's GiGi?"

"Hurting. Aunt Starla came by when she heard, then that brought over Serena. Grant just got here, so I thought I'd give you guys a call and let you know we decided to do an impromptu Sunday night dinner here in about thirty minutes if you can make it. Call Zoie and see if she can come as well."

"I think we can do that." I moved the phone from my mouth and told Alex what Mom had said.

He nodded. "I think we can take time for dinner as we wait to hear from Finn and Doc."

"We'll be there in five minutes," I told Mom. "Do we need to bring anything?"

"Just yourselves," Mom said before disconnecting.

I called Zoie, and before I said goodbye, she was already out the door headed to Mom's.

Alex parked behind Zoie's smart car in Mom's driveway. I

was happy to see there were no longer any reminders of the fire that had taken place at Mom's house just a few weeks before. Thankfully, Mom's house had been warded, so the fire only destroyed her lawn, a couple windows, her front bushes around the house, and some tiles on her roof. GiGi had performed a renewal spell for the front yard, so all Mom had to do was hire someone to replace the windows and fix the roof.

The front door opened, and Zoie greeted us. "Hey, Dad. Hey, Shayla. Everyone's in the kitchen. Poor GiGi is really upset."

It broke my heart to see GiGi sitting at the table, her eyes red and swollen. She gave us a weak smile when we walked into the room.

"Anything new?" she asked.

Alex shook his head. "No. We won't know anything more until we hear from Doc or Finn." He pulled out the chair next to GiGi. "I was hoping maybe you could shed some light on something her great-niece said. She told us Isaac Flowerbaum sent Selma a threatening letter. Do you know anything about that?"

GiGi's eyes widened. "I'd completely forgotten about that. But what she told me about wasn't a letter. She told me he stopped her coming out of the library one day—where she volunteers—and told her if she intended to make waves on some new project he was doing, then she'd regret it." GiGi frowned. "I really didn't get the full story, but I think maybe Isaac has to get permission from the City before he can build. Anyway, he pretty much tried to intimidate her." GiGi closed her eyes, then opened them. "That's really all I can think of. People don't normally try to muscle Selma. She was a kind woman. Led a pretty solitude life with her husband, Clarence, until he died. After he passed, she spent most of her time volunteering around the island. People liked Selma."

"Didn't Clarence's brother take Selma to court a few years ago?" Mom asked. "Something about a land dispute?"

GiGi nodded. "That's right. Nothing really came of it. Clarence's older brother, Niles, thought the family's land should revert to him when Clarence died, but Clarence had willed it to Selma. In the end, Selma kept the land."

"We'll speak with Niles Craftsman in the morning," Alex said. "He's a witch as well?"

"Yes," I said.

"I heard Selma was in awful shape," Aunt Starla said.

I shuddered. "It was horrible. I swear, it looked like something ate through half her face. But not with teeth marks. More like with acid."

Mom handed me a glass of white wine. I was about to wave it off, seeing as how I was technically still working, but then I thought, what the heck. I'd just witnessed something that deserved a drink.

"Are you thinking magic is involved?" Mom asked.

I shrugged. "I honestly don't know. I can't see how it wouldn't be, though."

Grant sat down at the table across from GiGi. "Anything you need me to do tonight, Alex?"

"If you're still here when we get the call to go down to the station," Alex said, "you're more than welcome to come with us. This way, you can hear what Doc and Finn have to say."

"I can do that," Grant said.

Mom softly clapped her hands. "Who's setting the table?"

Zoie waved a hand in the air. "Can I use magic?"

Mom chuckled. "You can."

As Zoie used her magic to set the table, I looked at Serena and frowned. "You not drinking any wine?"

Serena glanced at Grant, then shook her head. "Nope. Not tonight."

"And why is that?" I asked. "I've never known you to turn down a glass of wine."

Serena grinned and glanced again at Grant, raising her eyebrow.

Grant stood up from the table, sauntered over to Serena, and wrapped his arms around her waist, pulling her close. "I guess now's a good time to make our announcement."

Aunt Starla squealed. "Is it what I think it is?"

Serena's eyes filled with tears, and she let out a watery laugh. "I took a pregnancy test this morning for the second time this week. It's positive!"

A cheer went up in the kitchen, and even GiGi stood and did a little jig.

"How far along?" Aunt Starla asked.

"I think about nine weeks," Serena said.

Grant grinned. "It was a *really* good honeymoon."

We all laughed, and Serena smacked Grant lightly on the chest. "I didn't think anything about why I'd been so tired until after the Valentine's Day dinner party where you two got engaged. That night, after everyone left, I was dragging, but I shouldn't have been. That was my first sign something was up. I've been lucky, though. No morning sickness, just exhaustion."

Zoie handed Serena a glass of water. "While they do the adult toast, we can do the kid toast."

Mom and Aunt Starla poured more wine for everyone, and then Aunt Starla and GiGi both gave toasts. Afterward, Zoie asked to touch Serena's stomach, and GiGi started talking baby names.

I filled up on a hot roast beef sandwich, mashed potatoes,

asparagus, and a tossed salad. By the time I pushed my plate away, I thought for sure I was going to explode.

"Don't forget," Zoie said as she finished clearing the table. "Dinner is at Shayla's house Tuesday night. I'm making a leap year dinner."

I groaned. "Don't mention food."

Zoie giggled. "Sorry. I just didn't want anyone to forget."

"I have to ask," Alex said. "What kind of food gets served at a leap year dinner?"

Zoie waggled her eyebrows. "Foods you don't traditionally eat."

"You mean like snails and frog legs?" I asked.

Zoie laughed. "No. Well, I guess yes, you could do that, but I'm not going to. I mean like food you don't normally eat *together*. For example, fruit loop pancakes are on the menu, along with a couple other items."

I cocked my head to the side and frowned. "Seriously?"

Zoie huffed and threw her hands in the air. "Yes. This is why I didn't want to tell you. I wanted it to be a surprise. Trust me, you will all love what I'm going to fix."

I shrugged. "If you say so. I've tasted your food, and it's right up there with Serena's culinary skills."

"Mom," Aunt Starla said, "Serenity and I can take you to get the Lolly. Serenity can drive it back here for you."

"I'd like that," GiGi said.

"And don't worry," Mom joked, "I won't let GiGi sneak out later tonight and take the Lolly for a joyride."

Alex's phone rang, and the room went quiet.

"It's Doc." Alex answered, listened, then nodded. "Okay. We'll see you in about ten minutes."

5

G rant pulled his vehicle to a stop behind ours in front of the sheriff's station. The three of us quickly made our way inside the building and down the stairs. Since Pearl Earthly-Caraway wasn't behind the desk, we didn't have to talk our way past the dragon lady who usually guarded the front office like she was guarding treasure.

We hurried down the hall and stopped in front of Doc's laboratory. After a quick knock, Alex pushed opened the door, and we entered the sterile room. Finn was standing next to Doc at his new desk and computer.

"I think we have some leads for you," Doc said. "I'll go first, since Finn's report will really shed light on what I've discovered." He motioned us over to Selma's body and pulled back the sheet, exposing her upper half. "Cause of death was a heart attack, but I think we can all agree it was brought on by the acid-like attack she sustained to her face and neck. The rest of the autopsy was pretty straightforward. No alcohol or drugs in her system. She had strawberries, blueberries, and chamomile tea in her stomach, and was otherwise in great health for a witch her age." Doc nodded to Finn. "Go ahead."

Finn clasped her delicate hands in front of her. "The goo in the baggie is the same substance Shayla brought me last week, and the same Doc found on Selma's face and neck. It's an acid mixed with a secretion gel substance."

I nodded. "Right. That's what you said last week."

"How does that get us closer to identifying our killer?" Alex asked.

Finn held up a hand. "I believe it's how the—and hear me out here—how the plant is eating."

"Excuse me?" I mused. "The plant?"

Finn nodded. "The plant. The green item near the door I recovered from the scene came back as a plant specimen. More specifically, welwitschia or tree tumbo."

I gasped. "Welwitschia? That's the plant known as 'two leaves that cannot die,' isn't it?"

Finn nodded. "Yes."

Grant frowned and crossed his arms over his chest. "For those of us not up on plant speak, what are we missing?"

I thought about how best to describe the plant. "Think tumbleweed body with long, thick vines. The welwitschia is known for having two enormous leaves that grow from the base. These leaves can range from thirteen to twenty feet. And here's the crazy part—some plants are as old as two thousand years. That's why it's been given the name 'two leaves that cannot die.'"

"And it eats humans?" Alex asked.

I shook my head. "No. It doesn't really *do* anything. At one point, some tribes ate the core of the plant, but the plant itself doesn't offer medicinal uses or anything like that. It's just a cool plant."

"Where is it located on the island?" Alex asked me.

"I've only found two of them here on Enchanted Island so far in my cataloguing of the plants and animals on the north side. But understand, my primary focus this last year has been the north side of the island. It very well could be there are welwitschias located elsewhere, and I just haven't come across them yet. But I think it's important I tell you both the welwitschia plants on the north side are just plants. There's no magical quality to them."

"So you're thinking magic must be involved?" Grant asked.

I nodded. "Absolutely. If Finn found a piece of the vine at the crime scene, that means the plant is moving. That requires animation, and that requires magic. These plants don't move on their own."

"So someone is animating the welw—wella—whatever," Grant said, "to move around the island and eat animals and people?"

"I guess," I said. "I've discovered a couple animal carcasses over the last week, and now Selma. It makes sense to draw that conclusion. But I don't see how it's doing it. I mean, it's not like the welwitschia has an actual mouth or anything."

"Here's where my theory is going to get really insane," Finn said. "What if we're looking at a hybrid plant?"

"Whaddya mean?" I asked.

Finn sighed. "Some of the goo I have is the same substance found in the digestive enzymes secreted by the glands of a Venus flytrap, but like a thousand times stronger."

For a few seconds, no one said anything. We all just stared at Finn like she'd grown another head.

"Excuse me?" I said. "Are you saying we have a hybrid plant killer that has the body of a welwitschia and the head of a Venus flytrap?"

"That's what I'm saying," Finn said. "And the head would be enormous." She motioned to Selma's body. "Large enough to cover most of Selma, and it's using its vines to move around the island."

Alex shook his head. "This is surreal. But it explains a lot. Like why Shayla hasn't found teeth marks or claw marks on the eaten animals or Selma."

Grant ran a hand over his face. "So we're looking for a hybrid Venus flytrap who has a taste for human flesh. Great."

"We may need Black Forest King's help with this," Alex said.

I nodded. "We can go see Dad next."

Grant shoved his hands in his pockets. "I'll start research tomorrow and see if there have been any other cases like this in other supernatural towns."

"Why target Selma?" Doc mused. "Whoever is magically manipulating this hybrid plant to do its bidding, why go after Selma? I've never known her to have any enemies."

"We'll find out that answer," Alex said, "once we find our *true* killer."

* * *

Because it was getting late, and we were getting tired, Alex flew us out to Black Forest to see Dad. In a move I knew would get me in even more trouble later on, I elected not to stop by my castle first to let Needles know we were going to see Dad. I knew it would cost me dearly, but I did it anyway.

Entering Black Forest is utopia. At least, it is for me. It's almost indescribable—the overwhelming feeling of peace and tranquility mixed with the harmonious presence of the forest and the animals within. Just crossing over the threshold gave me a surge of power inside I could never explain—a boost of strength.

I'd recently discovered I could heal plants and animals by drawing on the power inside me that was part of Dad's DNA. Even though he never said it, I got the feeling I could do even more, but Dad was letting me spread my wings and discover things in my own time.

As Alex wound his way down to the ground, carefully avoiding the branches of the pine, oak, poplar, hickory, redwood, and myriad other mix of trees inside Black Forest, a gigantic ball of light came hurling our way.

"Right on time," Alex murmured in his deep, gravely gargoyle voice.

I laughed. "They're just excited to see us."

The ball of light scattered, and dozens of lightning bugs raced to us, each trying to beat out the other.

"It's lovely to see you both."

"Black Forest King was just talking about you today, Princess."

"Have you set a wedding date, Alex Stone?"

"Will you bring us sweet nectar next time you visit?"

On and on the questions went until Alex finally reached the forest floor and gently set me down next to Dad's tree before shifting.

My dad, a genius loci, was the tallest tree on Enchanted Island, with branches that extended out to forty feet. As a little girl, I used to climb them and lay for hours on his branches, either talking about my day or just reading a book.

"Hello, Daughter of my Heart." One of Dad's branches reached down and gently caressed my cheek, the leaves tickling my face. *"It is later than your usual visits. Is there a problem on the island?"*

"I'm afraid so," I said.

"Come, sit down. Needles is not with you, but I still have my connection to him, so I know it is not him. Same goes for your mother. Is it GiGi? Or Serena? Or Young Zoie?"

Alex and I settled on the ground at the base of Dad's trunk. I rested my back and head against the rough bark. "No, it's not immediate family. I'm afraid it's Selma Craftsman. GiGi and I found her today in her cottage. It's bad, Dad. I think it's the—well, I thought it was an animal or something I was tracking these last few weeks, but that's not it at all."

"Take your time, Shayla. Tell me what is bothering you tonight."

I reached down and clasped Alex's hand. "Okay. We have reason to believe a powerful witch or fairy on the island is using magic to wield a hybrid plant to kill. We believe the base of the hybrid plant is welwitschia, and the head is that of a Venus flytrap."

"And this hybrid plant is what has been eating some of the animals on the island, and has now killed Selma?"

"Yes. Have you ever heard of such a thing?" I asked. "Or do you know of a witch or fairy family who could yield power like that?"

"There are a few families who could wield that kind of power, if they wanted. I'm sure even GiGi could do it."

"We have two suspects," Alex said. "One is a witch, and the other a woodland fairy."

"It sounds like a good place to start," Dad said. *"I know Selma and GiGi were very close. She must be devastated."*

I blinked back tears. "She is. Whoever did this to Selma is evil. The Venus flytrap pretty much cut Selma in two. Ate away her face and neck. It was awful, Dad."

Another of Dad's branches came down and gently caressed

my shoulder. *"I will have the animals and trees watch out and be observant. If they come across this hybrid plant, I will have them notify me immediately. I will also use my power to see if I can try and make a connection with this hybrid plant and determine where it is."*

"Thanks, Dad."

"In the meantime," Dad went on, *"please be careful. This is not the act of a typical Venus flytrap. As I am sure you are aware, they only eat ants, spiders, and other small insects that land in their mouth. But I would agree, with the kind of power you are seeing, you are looking for a witch or a fairy."*

❦ 6 ❧

"**Y**ou owe me like three extra caramel-dipped pretzels," Needles whined as we got out of my Bronco in front of Enchanted Bakery & Brew around nine the next morning. *"Not only did I miss the discovery of a dead body, and the big announcement Serena is pregnant, but then you went and saw Black Forest King without me."* Needles' wings turned black. *"That's unforgivable, Princess."*

I rolled my eyes and opened the bakery's front door, inhaling the yummy smells and taking in the chatter of the customers. "Fine. I'll get you an extra pretzel. Sheesh. Will that make you finally stop whining?"

"I do not whine, Princess. I am a warrior. A protector of those less fortunate."

Needles zipped ahead of me to the display case, his wings now a vibrant red. A sure sign he was pissed.

"Good morning, Shayla," Serena called out from behind the counter.

"Morning, Serena." I eyed the cranberry-orange muffins Tamara carried out from the kitchen. "Those look delicious."

Tamara grinned. "Made fresh this morning."

I waved to Mom, Aunt Starla, and GiGi sitting in their usual spot near a window. I was about to place my order when I heard the bakery's door open. Turning, I smiled as Alex strode inside.

He leaned down and kissed my cheek. "Morning. You're looking sexy."

I snorted. "My hair is in a messy bun, I have on zero makeup, and I have on a tan and brown game warden uniform. How is that sexy?"

Alex winked. "Trust me, it is."

"If you two are done ogling each other," Needles said near my shoulder, *"I'd like to order."*

Alex grinned. "I take it he's angry?"

"How'd you guess," I grumbled.

"I can hear you both."

"Just like I can now, unfortunately, hear you," Alex said.

Not too long ago, Needles had been inside my Bronco when it exploded. Somehow, that incident broke the bonding connection Needles had with Dad and me, and made it so everyone who was at the accident site could now hear Needles speak. Something that drove Alex crazy.

After placing our order—cranberry-orange muffin with a large coffee for me, two caramel-dipped pretzels for Needles, and a cinnamon roll with a large coffee for Alex—and making small talk with local citizens, we carried our goodies over to where the rest of the family sat.

"How're you doing, GiGi?" I asked, taking a huge bite of my muffin.

"Still seems unreal," GiGi said, her eyes swimming with

tears. "Hard to imagine not hearing Selma's sweet voice ever again."

"We're heading out to see Niles now," I said. "Hopefully, we'll get this figured out soon."

Mom took a sip of her hot tea. "Were Doc and Finn able to shed light on this for you?"

I nodded. "We believe we are looking for a witch or fairy." I glanced around the bakery, not wanting anyone to overhear. "The rest will have to wait until later."

"I know Zoie usually cooks for you guys on Monday nights," GiGi said, "but since she's doing her leap year dinner tomorrow night instead, I thought you might like to stop by tonight on your way home, Shayla. I'm making homemade chicken noodle soup and naan bread."

"Sounds delicious," I said. "I'll text you when I get home tonight."

* * *

Niles Craftsman lived in the center of the island on thirty acres—I know because I had Grant check the court documents for me. If there was a dispute with the land, I wanted to know how much land we were talking about. In total, the family plot was sixty acres. Niles had inherited thirty acres plus the family house, while Clarence had inherited the other thirty acres.

Niles was sitting outside on his front porch with a brown hound dog snoring at his feet when we pulled to a stop in his yard. I guessed him to be in his nineties since he was Clarence's older brother.

"Mr. Craftsman?" Alex asked as we strode toward the porch.

"That's me. Why're you on my property? And what's that

thing flying around that girl's head?"

"I'm Sheriff Stone, and this is Agent Loci. The *thing* flying around her head is Needles."

Needles flew to the porch railing, yanked out two quills, and whipped them in the air. *"And if you don't want to lose a tongue, you'll watch how you speak to me, Witch!"*

"We'd like to talk to you about Selma Craftsman," I said.

"What about her?" Niles demanded.

"She's your sister-in-law?" Alex asked.

Niles shrugged. "Guess you could say that. She married my brother, but seeing as how he's dead, I don't guess we're in-laws now."

"When was the last time you spoke with Selma?" I asked.

"Dunno. It's been a while. I try not to speak to her unless I have to. The less I remind her I'm here, the less likely she is to do something stupid like sell my family's land."

"I heard about that," I said. "When your brother Clarence died, he left his thirty acres to Selma?"

"Yeah. Don't know why he did it. He *knew* that land should have gone to me. I was his brother, and this is our land. Been our land for more generations than I can count."

I nodded. "You sued Selma about five years ago. Is that right?"

"That's right. Not that it's any of your business."

"I don't like him," Needles said. *"He seems shifty and argumentative. My bet is he's the killer."*

"What's this all about?" Niles demanded. "Why're you asking questions about our land?"

"The questions are more about Selma than the land," I said. "Are you aware Selma Craftsman was murdered last night?"

Niles stopped rocking. "I was not."

"That got his attention." Needles flew to where the dog lay

motionless on the porch, then zipped back to the porch railing. *"Just making sure it was still breathing."*

I bit my lip to keep from smiling. "GiGi and I found Selma's body around four-thirty yesterday."

"You don't say?" Niles stood, and the dog at his feet whined but didn't move. "Murdered? How do you know?"

"Excessive trauma to her body," Alex said.

Niles walked over to the railing and scowled out at the surrounding trees. "What'll become of my brother's land now? Did she will *my* family's land to a stranger?" He whirled and glared at Alex. "This is ridiculous! The land my brother owned should now come to me."

"I'm not aware of what will happen to the thirty acres," Alex said coolly. "I'm sure Selma had a will that spells out her wishes."

"Damn unfair if you ask me." Niles crossed his arms over his sunken chest. "Don't think I won't fight the decision if I don't like it."

"I'm sure you will," Alex said. "Now, can you tell me where you were yesterday from four to four-thirty?"

"I was here. I'm ninety-two years old. It's not like I have an active social life anymore, Sheriff."

"Something tells me this guy never *had an active social life."* Needles did a somersault in the air. *"He's more of a repellant than an attractor."*

I choked back the laughter that threatened to escape. "Is there anyone who could verify you were home?"

"Just Petey." He pointed to the hound dog lying comatose at his feet.

I was half tempted to wake the dog and ask him if the alibi was true, but I didn't have the heart to wake the ancient hound.

"I'm curious," I said. "What did you do for a living, Mr.

Craftsman? Before you retired?"

"I was a landscaper," Niles said. "Why?"

"Ah-ha! Case closed." Needles stood and held out a paw. *"Give me your binder, Princess. I'll wrap this up right now."*

I gave Needles my best "enough" look before turning back to Niles. "Just curious. Did you ever infuse your plants with magic?"

Niles frowned, then shrugged. "I guess. I might give them a little extra boost to stay healthy, or maybe I used a little magic to create the perfect ambiance. Why?"

"Again, just curious," I said. "Do you think you could animate a plant?"

"Animate? You mean like make it come alive?" He scoffed. "Why would I wanna go and do that?"

"Oh, I don't know. Maybe to kill someone?"

"Could you, though?" I asked, doing my best to ignore Needles' crazy comments.

"I suppose," Niles said. "Not that I ever did."

"Do you know of anyone who might want to hurt Selma?" Alex asked.

"Like I told you earlier, I haven't spoken to Selma much since my brother died. Didn't care to after the fallout from the lawsuit. I know she volunteered some at the local library in town. Saw her there a couple times when I was going to the hardware store. Maybe someone in the library knows if Selma was making waves."

"Thank you for your time, Mr. Craftsman," Alex said.

"When you find out what'll happen to my land, will you let me know?" Niles asked.

"I doubt I'll find out," Alex said. "There would be no need for me to go to the will reading."

"But now I want to go," Needles said, his wings glowing

green and yellow. *"Especially if Selma did something crazy like donate the land to a daycare or something."*

Niles scowled. "No one better just drive up on my land one day next week and think they're gonna build on it or nothing like that. They won't like the outcome."

Alex rested his hands on his hips, emphasizing his gun. "And I'll tell you, Mr. Craftsman, that Selma has every legal right to will her land to whomever she wants. Unless you want me to come back out here and arrest *you*, I wouldn't go threatening anyone."

Needles mocked Alex's stance. *"Yeah. Don't make us come back out here, Niles. You won't like it."*

Once back inside the Blazer, I dug out my cell phone, called GiGi, and put her on speakerphone.

"Do you know if Selma had a will?" I asked.

"She did. Why?"

"We just spoke to Niles, and he's anxious about the thirty acres." I tossed Needles a pretzel. "You know anything about what'll happen to that land and her house?"

"Sure do," GiGi said. "Both her cottage and the five acres it was on—plus the thirty acres her husband left her—will go to the coven to do with as they see fit."

Alex chuckled. "Niles will have a fit."

"Good," GiGi said. "He's an old cranky-pants of a witch who needs his life shaken up a bit." There was a brief pause. "You think Niles killed Selma?"

"I don't know, GiGi," I said softly. "We're still interviewing people."

GiGi sniffed. "She was a good woman."

"I know." I said goodbye and disconnected.

"Library next?" I asked.

"I think so."

7

The Enchanted Island library was a two-story brick building located on the same street as The Craft & Candle and Forever Flowers. The library focused more on supernatural authors, but if you looked hard enough, you could find a non-supernatural author or two.

The one and only rule inside the library was that being quiet was forbidden.

Needles settled on my shoulder as Alex opened the door. Just like the last time I was inside the library, I was immediately bombarded with a cacophony of little kids' squeals and babble.

"Why's it so busy on a school day?" Alex asked.

I grinned as a boy of about three sat on a magic carpet, book in hand, and flew near the ceiling. "These kids are too young for school."

"Now that looks fun," Needles said. *"If I were a good hundred years younger, I might give it a try."*

Vivian Foxx, head librarian, looked up from behind her desk

and waved us over. I'd met Vivian, a fox shifter, months back on a different murder case.

"Hello, Sheriff and Shayla. And look, it's Needles!" She tucked a piece of red hair behind her ears, causing her thick stripe of white to show. "I wish I could say it was good to see you, but I know what this is about." Tears filled her eyes. "Poor Selma. She was such a loving and giving witch. All the kids loved when she'd volunteer to read to them. Do you know who hurt her?"

"We were hoping you might shed some light on that," I said. "Did she say anything to you about being threatened or scared recently?"

Vivian furrowed her brows in concentration. "You know? She sort of did. A couple days back, we were making small talk here at my desk before she was getting ready to leave. As she put on her coat to head outside, I told her to have a good night. She said something about hoping she could. When I asked what she meant, she said she thought someone was watching her."

"Did she say who?" I asked.

Vivian shook her head. "No. She just said she thought someone was watching her, and she also thought maybe someone had even gone onto her property."

"If you can think of anything else that might help us, please call." Alex handed her a card. "Have a good day."

I waited until we were outside to speak. "Something about what she said triggered me."

"What was that?" Alex asked.

"GiGi said she thought someone had been out by her cottage last week. I remember because she specifically called to ask if it was me."

"You think the same person who was watching Selma's house was watching GiGi's?" Alex asked. "But why?"

I shrugged. "I have no idea. But I don't like it."

Alex's cell rang as we hopped up inside the Blazer.

"Hey, Grant. What's up? Really? That's great. Gives us a place to start." He disconnected and started the engine. "I had Grant ask around today about the petition Selma had been circulating to stop the building of the bar. Seems if she was successful, it could cause Flowerbaum to lose thousands and thousands of dollars. Rumor has it the city council is split on how they might vote."

"Thousands of dollars? That's a huge motive," I said. "Are we going to talk with him next?"

"Before we do that, how about we stop for a late lunch? Then I want to go to Selma's place and see if we can't find that threatening letter. Give us the upper hand when we question Flowerbaum."

"Lunch sounds great," Needles said. *"I could go for a salty slice of ham."*

8

Isaac Flowerbaum lived in a two-story brick home on the east side of town. A tall, wrought-iron fence complete with a gated entrance barred us from driving up to the palatial estate. Alex pushed the button on the speaker box, and within seconds, a stuffy male voice answered.

"Good afternoon. How may I help you?"

Alex rolled his eyes at me. "Sheriff Alex Stone and Agent Shayla Loci to see Isaac Flowerbaum, please."

"One minute, Sheriff," the man said. "I will see if Mr. Flowerbaum is available."

"If he's home," Alex said, "he's available."

The man cleared his throat. "Yes, sir. Hold please. I'll let Mr. Flowerbaum know you are here."

Minutes later, a buzzer sounded, and the automated gate opened. "You may proceed to the house, Sheriff."

By the time we'd finished lunch, drove out to Selma's and searched through her things for the letter and any other clue we may have overlooked, then drove to Isaac's house, it was nearing four o'clock.

Alex parked in the circle drive, and we made our way up the cobblestoned walkway lined with shrubs and flowers. Before Alex could knock on the door, it opened to reveal a stern-looking man in a black suit.

"We need a butler for the castle," Needles said from my shoulder. *"Class up the place a little."*

"Never gonna happen," I hissed.

"I am Gerald. Mr. Flowerbaum will see you in his office." He motioned us inside. "Please, follow me."

I'd barely gotten in a cursory glance around the large foyer before Gerald stalked past a curved staircase and strode down a carpeted hallway. At the end of the hall, we took a left and stopped at an open door. Gerald bowed and motioned us inside.

"Come in." Isaac Flowerbaum stood from behind his desk and motioned us inside. "Please, have a seat."

When Alex and I did just that, Flowerbaum smoothed down his shirt and sat as well. "What can I do for the Enchanted Island police?"

"Do you know Selma Craftsman?" Alex asked.

Anger flashed in Flowerbaum's eyes. "Yes, I know her."

"Can you tell me how it is you know her?" Alex mused.

"Why is that important?" Flowerbaum picked up a pen and tapped it against the desk. "Did she file a complaint against me?"

"Did she have a reason to?" I asked.

"Selma Craftsman and I have what could be defined as a contemptuous relationship. She is angry at me and has, in fact, gone out of her way to try and smear not only my good name, but my company's name. Right this minute, she is circulating a petition to stop the growth of one of my projects." He set the pen down and smiled. "Can you imagine? I mean, this island needs to develop to compete with the other supernatural towns out there. When you build, jobs happen, and communities thrive. That's just a way of life."

"And Selma didn't want this growth?" I asked.

"She did not. She was more worried about local wildlife instead of helping the citizens of this island." He shook his head. "Sad really."

"Did you send a threatening letter to Selma?" Alex asked.

"I don't believe so."

Alex smiled and pulled out the letter we'd finally found and showed it to Isaac. "Maybe this will jog your memory."

"Busted!" Needles' wings glowed purple with glee. *"I love it when we catch suspects in a lie."*

Flowerbaum glanced down at the letter, then shrugged. "I guess maybe I did. I was just trying to convince her to see things my way. I wouldn't say it outright threatened her. I merely pointed out the many ways my bar would help the island. And I *may* have intimated she should see this as a good thing and back off with her petition."

"And if she didn't back off?" I asked. "What did you *intimate* then?" I tapped the letter on the desk. "It's in that paragraph, in case you forgot."

Isaac Flowerbaum narrowed his eyes at me. "Why don't you cut to the chase? Why are you *really* here?"

"Selma Craftsman was found murdered in her house yesterday," I said. "Your name came up as a person of interest. Does that clear things up for you?"

Flowerbaum let out a little laugh. "And you think *I* had something to do with her death? I can assure you, I didn't." He leaned forward and rested his elbows on his desk. "Selma Craftsman didn't worry me. Her petition didn't worry me. I know the men and women on the city council. There's no way they'd have given Selma's petition any merit. I had no reason to want her dead."

I crossed my arms over my chest. "Rumor has it if Selma was successful with her petition to stop your bar, you could lose thousands of dollars."

Flowerbaum shrugged. "Like I said, I wasn't worried."

His arrogance didn't sit well with me. "Rumor also has it a rather prominent coven of witches on the island are picking up where Selma left off." I gave him a tight smile. "So I guess you are right...we will see."

Flowerbaum lost his affable demeanor and narrowed his eyes. "I guess we will."

Alex crossed his arms over his chest. "I'd like to know your whereabouts for yesterday afternoon from three until five?"

Flowerbaum leaned back and studied Alex for a moment. "I'll do you one better. I'll give you my whereabouts for the whole day. I had breakfast here at my house, then left around ten to visit two of my building sites. After checking on the progress of both buildings, I came back home to work in my office. That was probably around one or so. I had dinner here and stayed in the rest of the night. Gerald can verify that for you."

"That's a little too convenient, Princess."

I had to agree with Needles on that. "Anyone else besides Gerald able to verify that alibi?"

Flowerbaum shrugged. "Sorry, no. I live alone except for Gerald. He has living quarters inside the house. I do have a housekeeper who comes once a week, but that's on Thursdays." He spread his arms wide. "I'm afraid you'll just have to take my word—and Gerald's word, of course." He stood and smoothed down his shirt. "Now, if you'll excuse me, I have a lot of work to finish today. I'm sorry about Selma Craftsman, but I didn't kill her. If you have any further questions, I can give you the name of my attorney." He scribbled down a name and phone number on a slip of paper and handed it to Alex. "You can go through him. That's all the time I have. Please see yourselves out."

I gave Flowerbaum a tight smile as I turned and strode out of his office. Inside, I was fuming. Nothing I hated more than being dismissed. Alex caught up with me in the foyer, but instead of saying anything, he just opened the front door for me.

"What do you think?" I asked once we were back inside the Blazer. "I mean, I know what *I* think about Flowerbaum personally, but what do you think about this alibi and motive?"

"Strong motive. Weak alibi."

I grinned. "My thoughts as well. Plus, he's a woodland fairy, so he can do magic."

"Why didn't you talk to the suit?" Needles asked. *"Maybe Gerald had something different to say?"*

"I don't think so," I said. "Gerald didn't strike me as an unsatisfied employee. He'd be paid well to verify Flowerbaum's alibi."

9

"Before we go home, I want to make a stop. The south side of the island is vast, and it's going to take me a while to comb this whole beachside." I turned off the main road out of town, and then made another right and turn onto an overgrown path most citizens didn't even know existed. "I won't be long."

"Are you sure this is even a road?" Needles whined as he bounced around in the front seat.

"Just hold on." I slid our windows down, and again silently thanked Weston for talking me into putting electric windows in my old Bronco the last time he fixed it. "It's going to get worse before it gets better." The road gradually narrowed, and soon we were deep inside a forest. "In fact, I may have to put it in four-wheel-drive before too much longer."

I continued bumping down the rocky lane, weaving between the trees. When the overgrown path finally gave way to no discernible road, I decided it was time to let the Bronco do what it does best.

"Why did you stop?" Needles asked, his wings glowing red and purple. *"What's wrong?"*

"Nothing. I just gotta lock down the hubs."

Now Needles' wings shimmered orange. *"Don't tell me we're going four wheeling?"*

I grinned. "Off-road at its best."

I hopped down from the vehicle and quickly locked the hubs. As I was about to step back inside, something grabbed my leg.

"Crap! I got vines coming at me!" I sent a bolt of magic to the vine around my calf, and it instantly let go—only to be replaced by another vine, and three more coming straight toward me.

"Needles! You need to hang on. When I get in, I'm gonna floor it." I zapped the vine around my ankle and all but levitated myself inside the Bronco. Shifting the vehicle into four-wheel-drive, I slammed my foot down on the gas pedal.

"I don't think this is a good idea!" Needles shouted, his wings now shimmering every color imaginable.

I yanked the wheel to the left, barely missing an oak tree. "If you think this is bad, you're going to hate this next part."

"Dare I ask?"

"We're about out of trees. Next comes the ocean."

I glanced in my rearview mirror and saw the vines still chasing us. When one of them wrapped around my bumper and yanked it off, I cursed. "I just got this damn vehicle fixed *again*! This means war!"

"Plan your retaliation later, Princess," Needles hissed. *"We got trouble ahead."*

He was right. The forest was widening and getting brighter. Soon we'd be out of the trees—which meant we were less than twenty yards from the sand and water.

"I have a plan," I said.

Needles groaned. *"Why don't I like the sound of that."*

"Just do as I say. When I tell you to, I want you to take the wheel and steer."

Needles' his mouth dropped. *"Are you insane? Do you forget I'm the porcupine, Princess? I can't drive! I don't have hands! And I sure the heck can't reach the pedals!"*

"Dial it back," I snapped. "I'll run the pedals, you steer. Your paws can steer us straight. I have to be able to take out the vines. If I don't, the water is the least of our problems. Something tells me these vines will consume the Bronco with us inside."

I didn't pay attention to the words Needles mumbled under his breath. Instead, the minute our tires touched the sand, I shoved my hand out the window and whispered a spell. Seconds later, the air in the tires released.

"We're sinking!" Needles shouted.

"We're not sinking. Not now, anyway. If I hadn't let some of the air out, we might have." I yanked the wheel to the left and drove as fast as I could on the sand. "We are now running parallel to the main road. We can drive straight for miles and miles and be okay."

"So then you drive," Needles said.

"I can't! I have all these vines to kill." I cursed as a vine slithered up the back window. "Get ready to take over driving."

Scooting until I was as close to the driver's side door as possible, I whispered the levitated spell and levitated myself up onto the window ledge, sticking the upper half of my body out of the Bronco—all the while, keeping my foot on the gas pedal.

"Okay, Needles! You're driving!"

I let go of the wheel as Needles flew to me. Twisting so I could face the back of the Bronco, I zapped a vine near the back tires.

"I'm demanding a raise! I don't get paid enough for this. I'm a warrior, not a dune buggy driver!"

Rolling my eyes, I waited until a vine that had crept up the back was now partway across the roof of the vehicle. Once I had it in my sight, I gave it a zap of magic, and it immediately snapped apart, withered, and died.

"How much longer?" Needles shouted as the wheel made a sudden right—heading straight for the water and nearly tossing me out the window.

"Only two more vines," I snapped, reaching in and straightening the wheel. "Try to keep from killing us. "

"Easy for you to say!" Needles shouted, his wings throwing off myriad colors. *"I don't know why I couldn't be the one to do the zapping."*

"Because you don't have that magical ability." I took careful aim and snapped another vine in half. "Or is your memory going in your old age?"

"I'd laugh, but I need to focus on driving—words I never thought I'd speak in my life!"

Laughing, I slid back inside the Bronco and grabbed the wheel. "How about I let you do the honors of taking out the last vine?"

Needle snorted as he flew to the passenger-side window. *"Let me guess? You couldn't reach it from where you were?"*

I grinned. "Guilty. Do me a favor—don't get yourself killed."

Wings shimmering red, Needles yanked two quills out of his back and zipped out the window. I slowed down just a fraction and glanced in the rearview mirror. Needles whipped his two quills in rapid succession, dropping the vines onto the sand.

"No more killer vines headed our way, Princess." Needles settled back down onto the passenger seat.

"Wonderful. And see, driving isn't really that hard."

47

Needles glared at me, his wings still glowing a fiery red. *"For the record, I never want to drive again."*

I threw back my head and laughed. "Duly noted."

10

Needles elected to stay at the castle and keep guard there instead of going with me to eat supper with GiGi. Of course, I knew the "keep guard" was just an excuse. He was still pretty shaken up from the chase. No one really ventured out this way enough that Needles ever had to watch over the house.

Only one person had ever disregarded the rules surrounding our land and trespassed to dump a dead body. Tyler Stryker—a Normal who ended up trying to place the blame on his old brother, Dash. It was the first case I'd worked when I returned to the island over a year ago. It was also the first time I'd met Alex and Zoie.

"Be back later," I called out to Needles as I zipped my runner's jacket and jogged out the front door.

Instead of taking a right like I normally would when visiting Dad in Black Forest, I made a left and started back down our lane. GiGi's place was a little less than a mile away.

When we'd arrived home, I'd called Alex to tell him what had happened. He promised to fly out to the area and retrieve my bumper and drop it off at Weston's Auto Body for Weston. The mole shifter could pay off his house from my services alone, but he was worth it. On more than one occasion, he'd worked magic on my Bronco.

The sun was about to set when I opened GiGi's front door. The scent of chicken noodle soup permeated throughout her small cottage, and I relished in the nostalgia of my childhood. This was my favorite meal GiGi would prepare when I was younger—complete with either homemade French bread or naan.

"GiGi?" I called out. "You in the kitchen?"

GiGi popped her head out from the doorway on the left. "Just about ready. I opened a pinot to go with the soup."

I laughed. "Chicken noodle soup and wine. I'm in."

Dinner was delicious, and once the leftovers were put away and the dishes washed and dried, GiGi and I topped off our glasses and went to the living room to talk.

"It's been a while since we did this," GiGi said.

"I know. This last year has been such a whirlwind. Alex and I dating. Zoie learning magic and then coming into her own by discovering she's also a gargoyle. Mom and Dad finally talking after all these years." I gave GiGi a grin. "*You* and Dad talking after all these years. Plus, Grant and Serena dating, and then getting married, and now having a baby."

GiGi clinked my glass with hers. "That one makes me the happiest."

I laughed. "I know. A new baby will be…amazing."

"Our family legacy will live on. I was beginning to worry."

I rolled my eyes. "I don't know why. Serena has always wanted children."

"And you? If Zoie is all you and Alex have, will you be happy?"

I thought about that for a moment. "Yeah. I can honestly say if Alex and I choose to keep things as they are, I can be satisfied with that. Zoie is a great kid. Soon, she'll be a great adult." I laughed. "Who knows, in five or ten years, I may be a grandmother!"

GiGi grinned. "Best gig ever."

"How're you holding up?" I whispered, patting her knee.

"Not well. I'm just so sad. Such a useless tragedy." She took a huge swallow of her wine. "You find out anything useful?"

"Maybe. Since Selma volunteered at the library, Alex and I went to talk with Vivian Foxx, the librarian. She said Selma told her last week she thought someone was watching her. Not only that, Selma thought someone had been on her property."

GiGi sat up straighter and frowned. "Like me?"

"Like you."

"That's weird. Do you think the killer watched me because he or she knows Selma and I are—were friends?"

I shrugged. "I don't know. What would be the purpose? Of our two suspects so far—Isaac Flowerbaum and Niles Craftsman—neither one of them would gain anything by watching you. And why risk it? I mean, everyone knows this land is off limits because it's so close to Black Forest. Why would either man chance something like that just to watch you?"

"You're right. It doesn't make sense. What about the *thing* doing the killing? Have you seen any more evidence of it on the south side of the island?"

"No, but you're talking about miles and miles and miles of beaches and forests to search." I finished off my wine. "There is something I haven't told you yet. We believe the *thing* responsible for the killings is a hybrid plant—part welwitschia and part Venus flytrap."

"What!" GiGi sat up straight. "Are you *serious*? You're

talking species crossing and animation. That's some major magic going on."

I nodded. "I know. Think Flowerbaum or Craftsman are capable of that?"

GiGi frowned. "I'm not sure. I would think Flowerbaum has the best chance since he's a woodland fairy, but I can't say for sure. Are these two your only suspects?"

"For now. They both have motives."

"But?" GiGi prompted.

I shrugged and looked down at my empty wineglass. "But something is bothering me about the spying. Why would these men spy on you? Doesn't make sense."

GiGi nodded. "It's smart to keep your mind open to other possibilities." She patted my leg. "It's getting late. You want any soup to take home with you?"

I shook my head and stood. "No. I'm sure I'll have leftovers from Zoie's meal tomorrow night." I laughed. "Leap year dinner. Have you ever heard of anything so strange?"

"The girl is a gem." GiGi kissed me on my cheek and took my wineglass. "You go on home. You look exhausted."

"Thanks. Dinner was amazing."

The temperature had dropped another ten degrees in the hour and a half I'd been inside GiGi's cottage. That second helping of soup and second glass of wine didn't seem like such a smart choice now that I needed to jog home. Kicking myself for my bad choice, I took off at a brisk walk—only to stop midstride a couple yards later.

Something didn't feel right. The hairs on the back of my neck and on my arms were telling me I wasn't alone. Glancing around, I scanned the woods for something unfamiliar.

"Of all the times to wish I had Needles with me," I muttered. "He could at least fly around and see an aerial view."

I was about to call out to the rabbit scampering ahead of me along the path, but I hesitated. If the hybrid plant *was* somewhere near, no sense sending the defenseless rabbit to its death. Ignoring the protest of my full stomach, I took off for my castle at a steady jog, hating the fact that for the first time ever, I was actually nervous to be out in my woods.

🦋 11 🦋

I woke up exhausted and alone in the house—except for Needles, that is. Usually Alex and Zoie spent the night on Monday nights, but since Zoie was having her big dinner party at my place later, she'd elected to stay in town and prep last night. I'd tossed and turned most of the night, worried about GiGi and how she was taking Selma's death, the unknown visitor at her place last week, and about the weird feeling I had walking home last night.

By the time I dressed and dragged myself into town and parked in front of the bakery, I was itching for some of Serena's magical coffee.

"I've been thinking about what kind of crazy food Zoie might make tonight." Needles stopped in front of the bakery door and waited for me to open it. *"I may need you to stock up on extra pretzels and caramel. Just in case I need an emergency stash."*

"Nice try. But you aren't getting more than your normal one pretzel."

Needles' wings turned red, and he tried his best to cross his short front paws over his chest. *"You'd rather I starve to death?"*

Laughing, I opened the bakery door. "I'm willing to chance it."

When I stepped inside, I came up short. GiGi was sitting at a table with Mom and Aunt Starla. Forgoing my coffee for another minute, I hurried over to their table.

"What're you doing here?" I asked GiGi.

"I didn't sleep well, so I called my daughters and invited them to breakfast this morning."

"And how did you get here?" I hissed.

"I drove the Lolly into town."

I groaned and glanced over at Alex ordering at the counter. "If Alex finds out you drove to town by yourself without a license, he's going to arrest you! You understand that, right?"

GiGi grinned. "I'd like to see him try."

"Try what?" Alex asked as he sidled up next to me carrying a large white bag and two coffees. He handed me one of the coffees. "I'm surprised to see you here so early, GiGi. If you didn't ride in with Shayla, how did you get to town?"

"I picked her up," Aunt Starla and Mom both said simultaneously.

I groaned.

Mom laughed. "What we meant to say was *we* picked GiGi up and brought her to town."

"Uh-huh." Alex narrowed his eyes at GiGi. "I better not find out you drove into town without a license."

"Then you better not drive by Serenity's house," GiGi quipped. "Because you won't like what you see, Sheriff."

"GiGi's gonna get arrested!" Needles exclaimed excitedly, his wings glowing green.

"GiGi," Alex growled. "How can I be expected to uphold the law on this island if you won't—"

"I got some news," GiGi interrupted. "Something that might help you with your investigation."

Alex sighed and shook his head. "And what's that?"

GiGi took a sip of her hot tea. "I got a call about midnight last night from Lolita Herbton."

Surprised, I slid my gaze to Mom. Getting a call from Lolita was big news. "Really? What did she say?"

"Who's Lolita Herbton?" Alex asked.

"She's an oracle witch," GiGi said.

"And what's that exactly?" Alex asked.

"She can sometimes see the future—visions," GiGi said. "Anyway, she called and said she couldn't sleep. Had a bad feeling. She was going to go outside and consult the stars and moon to see what they had to say. She wanted me to stop by later today to discuss what she discovered, but I'm thinking this might be more up your alley." GiGi shook her head. "She said there was a darkness over the island."

"We can do that," I said. "Does she still live on the south side of the island by the old inn?"

"She does," GiGi said.

"Be safe," Mom said. "We'll see you guys tonight for Zoie's leap year dinner party."

"Three more weeks until spring." Aunt Starla sighed. "I can't wait. This island needs some newness and rebirth."

"So where is this old inn?" Alex asked once we exited the bakery and hopped inside his Blazer. "I take it it's no longer open?"

"It closed down about two hundred years ago," I said. "It's still standing, just abandoned. Outside of the Enchanted Island

Museum, it was my favorite place to hang when I was a teenager. I used to pretend I could still see and hear people inside."

Alex grinned. "I'm not at all surprised."

"She was always a little strange," Needles said. *"You might want to remember that if you guys decide to have kids after you're married."*

I turned and glared at Needles. "That's rich coming from a talking and flying porcupine."

Needles grinned, caramel dripping from his chin. *"Jealous?"*

I rolled my eyes and turned back around. "He's incorrigible sometimes."

"Sometimes?" Alex mused.

"I heard that, Gargoyle."

"I found your bumper and dropped it off at Weston's Auto," Alex said. "He told me to tell you he'd call with a time to put it back on."

"Thank you."

We drove the rest of the way in silence. When Alex came to the turnoff where the inn used to be, I told him to take a left. We bumped along the gravel road for about five minutes until we came to a three-sided stone structure with no roof, and a beautiful hickory tree growing out of the center.

"That's the old inn?" Alex asked, slowing down.

"That's it. Back in the day, it had a tavern and kitchen up front, a place for the owner in the back to live, and four bedrooms up on the second floor." I pointed to a structure in the distance that was now just two poles in the ground. "That used to be where the travelers could keep their horses."

"Nice bit of history," Alex said.

"I agree. I'm glad it's still standing, even after all these years."

Alex drove past the dilapidated stone building and continued driving until the surrounding trees seemed to close in on us.

"Up here a little farther," I said, "there'll be a fork in the road. We need to take the right."

"Is it me, or is the road getting narrower?" Alex asked.

"It's getting narrower."

Hearing soft snores behind me, I turned and smiled at Needles—head rolled to the side, eyes closed, and still gripping half his gooey pretzel in his right paw.

"Sugar puts him out every time," I said.

Alex curved to the right and slowed down to a snail's pace. I couldn't believe Needles could sleep through all the tossing and bumping.

"There it is," I said, pointing to a spot between two trees. "Careful. The branches are so long, they might scrape the side of the Blazer. We may need to walk."

"I think it'll be okay."

We squeezed through the last of the trees and came out in a small clearing where Lolita's cottage stood—or where Lolita's cottage *should* have stood. Only a third of the house was now visible.

"What's going on?" I asked, hopping out of the vehicle before it even came to a stop. "It looks like vines have eaten her house. The *same* vines that chased me last night."

"Kudzu." Alex shut off the engine and joined me near the hood. "Aggressive. When's the last time anyone was out here?"

I shrugged. "Not sure. Maybe a couple months for GiGi."

"Kudzu is fast growing," Alex said. "About a foot a day. But even at that rate, there's no way her cottage should look like this in just a couple months."

"I can't even see her front door," I said. "And seeing as how she just spoke to GiGi last night, I can't imagine her cottage looked like this yesterday. Dad's gonna be livid. Kudzu is the only plant not allowed on the island because it destroys everything it touches."

Alex whipped out his gun. "Be on guard."

Nodding, I crept to where I knew the front door should be, and using magic, I conjured up a machete.

"Nice," Alex murmured.

Grinning, I sliced through the vines. "Gets the job done."

When I finally had the front door exposed, I turned the handle and pushed my way inside. Just like the outside, the inside walls and floors were also partially covered in kudzu. Climbing over the vines, we made our way into the kitchen.

"Lolita?" I called. "Are you here?"

Silence.

"I have a bad feeling about this," Alex said.

"Me too."

"Bedroom or outside?" Alex asked.

"Let's see if she's outside, since that's where she was supposed to go last night to consult the stars and moon."

I pushed through the last of the vines and yanked open the back door. Stepping out onto the back deck, I gasped when I saw Lolita Herbton sprawled out on the ground, her lower half covered in kudzu vines while her face and neck had the same acid-like bite burns as Selma. Lolita was inches from entering the protection circle she had erected.

We ran toward the body, Alex still surveying the area with his gun. I knelt down next to Lolita and examined her wounds. "Same gooey substance."

"I read up on Venus flytraps last night," Alex said, holstering his gun. "If they get something inside their mouth that's not an insect or something they can't eat, they will immediately open their mouth. I think that's what is happening here. This hybrid plant knows it can't digest what's in its mouth, so it lets it go. But by that time, the acid has done its job and eaten through the flesh."

I shuddered. "Poor Lolita." I looked inside the circle and frowned. "It looks like she was able to get something inside the protection circle before it killed her."

"Can you get it?" Alex asked. "I mean, if it's inside a protection circle, and the person who made it is dead, how can you get what's inside?"

"Depends on what she erected. Could be she knew what was coming for her and made it to keep that entity out." I stood and neared the circle. "Only one way to find out." Taking a deep breath, I laid the machete on the ground, then carefully slid my foot across the threshold and inside the circle. When I wasn't met with a barrier or given a jolt, I inched the rest of my way inside the circle.

"What is it?" Alex asked as I picked up the item on the ground.

"Looks like a journal." I groaned. "She wrote down that something was taking the witches, and that GiGi is next. And that we should look to the past."

"Look to the past?" Alex mused. "What exactly does that mean?"

"I'm not—"

"Look out, Princess!" Needles screamed as he zipped around the front of the house, two quills swinging in the air as his wings glowed red. *"Move! Move!"*

I screamed when a large kudzu vine lifted itself off the cottage and grabbed Needles around one paw, yanking him to a halt.

"It's got me!" Needles yelled, his wings turning black and gray. *"Save yourself, Princess!"*

Shoving the journal down the front of my shirt, I snatched up the machete.

"Get to the vehicle!" Alex yelled as two vines reached out and tugged him to the ground. Shifting to his gargoyle form, he reached out and swiped at the vines with his sharp talons.

I'd almost reached Needles, when a kudzu wrapped itself around my left arm and right ankle, nearly ripping me in half. Pushing down the pain, I reached over and sliced through the vine wrapped around my arm, then bent down to cut myself free at the ankle.

"Let's go!" Alex cried in his gravely gargoyle voice. "We need to get away from here."

He carefully grabbed me by my shirt, causing me to drop the machete, and yanked me along beside him. As we neared Needles—now lying on the ground, almost entirely covered in the vines—Alex reached down and slashed the vines away from Needles' body, picked him up, tossed him to me, then shifted to human form.

We ran like the devil himself was chasing us. Yanking open the passenger-side door, I pitched Needles onto the floorboard and hopped up inside as Alex started the vehicle, put the Blazer in reverse, and floored it.

Hoping to take my mind off the fact we could smack into a tree at any given moment flying backward like we were through the thick forest, I gently picked up Needles and cradled him in my lap.

"You okay?" I conjured up a pair of scissors and cut away the vines. "Hurt anywhere?"

"Just my pride, Princess."

I smiled. "Join the club. I can't believe I didn't see the attack coming."

"None of us did," Alex said as he slowed the vehicle down

and turned it around to face the correct way. "The more impor-tant question here is who is controlling the hybrid plant and kudzu? And who hated these witches enough to kill them?"

"And why is GiGi next?" I demanded.

"I think I need some salt," Needles said, standing in my lap and giving his quills and wings a good shake. *"And a nap."*

I chuckled as he flew to the backseat. "Are we bringing someone out here to process the scene?"

"No. I don't think it's safe just yet. I want to see what Black Forest King has found out."

"Sounds good," I said. "I could use the calming he brings me after that death-defying escape."

12

A lex pulled into my yard twenty minutes later. I'd called Doc to let him know about Lolita, but left strict instructions not to retrieve the body until Alex deemed it safe.

"Do you want to run or fly to Black Forest?" Alex asked.

"Fly."

Even though Dad's place was only about a mile from my castle, and I loved jogging through the forest trail to see him, I didn't think we had that kind of time to waste.

"I sent a message letting him know we were coming in," Needles said before he zipped ahead of us.

Shifting into his gargoyle form, Alex spread his wings and gathered me in his arms. I smiled and held on tight as he sprang into the air, the lift causing my bangs to move over my forehead.

We'd just crossed into Black Forest when the fireflies came.

"Something is wrong, Princess!"

"Black Forest King is worried!"

"Will you be safe?"

My heart breaking at their anguish, I tried to divert their attention.

"I have news," I said.

"What?"

"Tell us, Princess!"

"You've set a date for the wedding?"

I laughed. "No, we haven't set a date. But Serena is going to have a baby!"

A dozen or so fireflies let out squeals of joy.

"A baby!"

"We haven't had a baby since Serena."

"Is it a boy or a girl?"

"It's still too early to know," I said as Alex slowly made his way to the forest floor.

"Go away!" Needles shooed. *"We have a lot to discuss with Black Forest King."*

The lightning bugs zipped away, chattering amongst themselves as I ran up Dad's roots.

"I fear you bring alarming news, Daughter of my Heart," Dad said. *"What has happened now?"*

"Alex and I went to see the oracle witch, Lolita Herbton." I sighed and sat down, leaning against his trunk. "She was dead. It looks like she tried to get inside a protection circle she made, but she didn't make it. Not only that, but her cottage was covered in kudzu."

"That is a plant I do not allow on the island. It grows too fast and kills everything in its path. It could consume a forest in no time."

"I know."

Alex cleared his throat and sat down next to me. "That is not the worst of it, sir. As we were examining the body, it was as if the kudzu came alive and tried to kill Needles, Shayla, and me."

The ground under me shook, and Dad's branches swayed. I laid my palm against Dad's trunk. "It's okay, Dad. We weren't hurt."

For a few seconds, no one said anything—and when I say no one, I mean even the trees and animals seemed to hold their breath waiting to hear from Black Forest King.

"I have been concerned, but not worried. That has now changed. Last night, something happened I cannot explain. I pulled on my connection with the island like I do countless times a day, and for the first time ever...I felt dead spots."

"What's that mean?" I asked.

"I am not sure how to explain, Shayla. It is like dead pockets —nothing moving or growing. It is something I have never experienced before. The island is always growing and shifting. There is always life on the ground. That is the magic of Enchanted Island."

"Kudzu?" Alex mused. "Could that be what's cutting you off from parts of the island?"

"It could be. Eating everything in sight and killing parts of the land. You must stop it, Shayla."

"I will, Dad." I grabbed hold of Alex's hand. "*We* will. Not only will we find the witch or fairy who's doing the killing, but we'll also stop him or her from killing any more of the island with the kudzu."

"I know you both will, Shayla. But please do it quickly."

"There's one more thing," I said. "The oracle witch managed to save a journal inside the circle. It basically said someone was killing witches, that GiGi was next, and we must look to the past."

"You must protect GiGi, Shayla. If anything were to happen to her, your mother would be devastated."

"I know," I whispered.

"The oracle said to look to the past, sir," Alex said. "Can you think of any family from generations past who would want to hurt witches on the island?"

"Anything you can tell us would be helpful, Dad," I added.

There have been inhabitants here on Enchanted Island for nearly four hundred years. I am sure there are some families who left the island in disgrace or anger. I will think on this, Daughter of my Heart. When I have an answer, I will communicate through Needles.

* * *

"Now what?" I asked when we dropped into my front yard ten minutes later.

"Did Lolita have a next-of-kin?" Alex asked.

"I think so. Let me check with GiGi."

"Don't tell her yet what the oracle wrote," Alex cautioned. "Let's do that face-to-face over lunch at your mom's. I'll call Grant and have him meet us at Serenity's house as well. See what he's found out about murders like this in other supernatural towns."

It was a difficult call to make. When I told GiGi about Lolita, she cried. No surprise there. I felt a twinge of guilt over not telling her about the oracle's premonition, but Alex was right… we needed to tell GiGi to her face.

"Her daughter's name is Athelia Briarwolf," I said as I disconnected and hopped inside the Blazer. "She lives in town."

"Black Forest King is right," Needles said, settling into the backseat. *"We need to find this wielder of evil and take them out."*

It was a quiet ride back into town—the three of us lost in our own thoughts. As we pulled into Athelia's driveway, I tried to calm the nerves bouncing around inside me. I couldn't get the fact GiGi was next out of my head.

"I'll stay in the vehicle," Needles said from the backseat. *"You know I hate this part of the job."*

Athelia Briarwolf didn't look a day over fifty, even though I knew she was closer to seventy. Her strawberry-silver hair, cut in a chin-length bob, was a pleasant contrast to her sharp, blue eyes. When she opened the front door, she immediately went from friendly to horrified.

"Oh, no! I knew something was wrong! I've been trying to reach Mom all morning. I've just had this horrible feeling." She reached out and braced herself against the doorjamb. "Just tell me."

Alex took a deep breath. "I'm afraid we have bad news. Your mother, Lolita Herbton, was killed either late last night or early this morning. Agent Shayla Loci and I were the ones to find her."

Athelia doubled over, and a long, mournful wail filled the air. "No. Why? Who did this?"

Alex helped her straighten and gently guided her inside. I stepped in behind them and shut the door.

"I'm sorry for your loss," Alex said. "Is there anyone we can call for you?"

Athelia shook her head. "No. I'm an only child, and Mom's brother passed away about ten years ago. There is no one but my own children to tell, and I will do that." She wiped the tears from her face. "My husband should be home for lunch any minute now. I'll tell him when he gets here." She sat down in a recliner and motioned for us to sit on the couch. "Please tell me what happened."

"We don't have much to tell right now," Alex said. "Your mother contacted Shayla's grandmother last night and asked to speak to GiGi later today after consulting the stars and moon.

GiGi thought it would be best if Shayla and I went to speak to her because—well, because of other incidents around the island."

"It's okay. You can speak freely. I know something is going on. Mom's been worried for almost two weeks now. She kept telling me someone evil was here, and that something was lurking beyond the shadows. Something dark. Something she couldn't see. Which was odd, because Mom could usually discern her visions. But for some reason, she couldn't see what was here on the island."

Alex nodded. "When Shayla and I arrived, we found your mother in her backyard."

"It looked like she'd erected a protection circle," I said, "but she didn't make it inside. We could retrieve a journal she'd placed in the circle, though."

"That's not all," Alex said. "When we arrived, your mother's cottage had been completely overrun with kudzu. Only a small portion of her house was visible to us."

Athelia gasped. "Is that what killed Mom?"

Alex shook his head. "Like I said, we can't be certain of anything. As Shayla and I went to examine your mother's body, the kudzu—well, it's like it came to life and attacked us. We had to fight our way out. I have informed Doc Drago what has happened, but until we get control of the kudzu, I can't let anyone near the house."

Athelia's hands covered her mouth, and for a few seconds, she didn't say anything. Lowering her hands, she placed them against her heart. "Are you saying my mom is still lying outside?"

Alex closed his eyes. "I'm sorry. Yes. It's too dangerous right now to try and extract her."

"Oh, my goddess. Why is this happening?"

"We were hoping you might know," I said. "Did Lolita give

you any idea who she thought might be here on the island wanting to hurt her?"

"No." She leaned forward, dropping her hands between her knees. "Does this have to do with Selma Craftsman's death as well?"

"We think so," I said. "Did your mom mention a link between certain witches on the island and maybe someone from the island's past?"

Athelia shook her head. "No. Like I said, she just kept saying someone was here, and that something evil was on the island."

"Please do not go to your mother's house until we have it secured," Alex said. "I have a team gathered to meet at your mom's later this afternoon. I'll call you when we've been able to…" Alex's voice trailed away. "I'll contact you and let you know when Doc says it's okay for you to come in and see your mother, if you'd like?"

Athelia stood and wiped more tears from her cheeks. "I would appreciate that, Sheriff."

13

"We know what we're looking for," I said, setting a platter of sandwiches on Mom's kitchen table. "We just don't know who is controlling it."

"Why do I get the feeling there's more to this story?" GiGi pulled out a chair and sat down. "What aren't you saying?"

Mom handed Needles two large pretzel sticks before carrying a pitcher of tea to the table. "Just let Shayla finish, Mom."

GiGi harrumphed and grabbed the bowl of fruit salad. "I'm trying to be patient, but she's taking forever."

Grant grinned and grabbed a sandwich, while Alex winked at me.

"As I was saying," I said tightly, "we know what we're looking for, just not who." I snatched a sandwich from the tray. "And, yes, there is more." I took a nibble, trying to bide my time. "Lolita had made a protection circle, but couldn't get inside in time. However, she *was* able to throw a journal in the circle. It's been bagged for evidence, but it basically said something was coming for the witches, and that GiGi is next." I cut my eyes to GiGi. "And that we should look to the past."

Mom gasped. "Lolita predicted GiGi would be next?"

"Simmer down," GiGi said. "This is good news." She took a drink of her tea before continuing. "We know this maniac's next move. He wants me...he can come get me."

I rolled my eyes. "I think we need to focus on the past prediction. What witch or fairy family on the island from generations past would have a grudge against—well, against the island's most powerful witches? Because that's who it seems this person is targeting."

"What do the three of you have in common?" Alex asked.

"Outside of the coven, not much. I mean, Lolita was a good twenty or more years older. Selma and I grew up together on the island, so there's that connection. You think the killer is targeting witches in the founding families' coven?"

"That seems to be the common thread," Alex said.

"We need to check the old books," GiGi said. "I'll have Starla meet me and your mom at my cottage around two this afternoon. The three of us will do a vision spell, and then we'll bring the leather-bounds to your place, Shayla. We can pour over them tonight after dinner."

"What's a vision spell?" Alex asked.

GiGi tossed a strawberry into her mouth. "It's a spell that will make us alert to the truth as we read the old scrolls in the leather-bound books."

Alex turned to Grant. "What about you? Did you find out anything this morning?"

Grant shook his head. "Not really. Nothing popped for past cases with Venus flytrap killing. I've checked the database from eight different paranormal towns so far, but no hits."

* * *

"**I** think I'll call Zane and see if he's heard of a witch using hybrid plants to kill," I said as Alex drove out to Lolita's cottage.

Zane was my partner back when I worked as a detective for PADA—the Paranormal Apprehension and Detention Agency. His new partner, Kara Hilder, was a Valkyrie who once worked with Alex back in Seattle.

Zane picked up on the third ring. "This is Zane. How are you, Shayla?"

I put him on speakerphone. "Hey, Zane. I'm good, thanks. We have a weird case here on the island. I don't suppose you've heard of a witch or fairy who uses hybrid plants to do his or her killing have you?"

"Can't say I have," Zane said. "What kind of plant are we talking?"

"A welwitschia's body and a Venus flytrap head."

Zane whistled. "Brutal. How many have died?"

"I have two witches dead, and according to the oracle witch who was just murdered, GiGi is next."

Zane cursed softly. "I haven't heard of anything like this, but I'll call PADA and see what I can find out."

"Thanks, Zane." I cleared my throat. "I owe you one."

"You just make sure you keep that sassy GiGi safe."

"I will." I disconnected and shoved the phone inside the pocket of my uniform. "Hopefully, we'll learn something from PADA."

We bumped along the rutted path until we couldn't go any farther. Stepping out of the Blazer, I turned to see Grant's and Doc's vehicles pulling to a stop behind us and parking. Finn waved as she stepped out of Doc's van.

"I'll stay here like last time," Needles said, *"and keep an eye out for any kudzu or hybrid plant on a mission to kill."*

"I can't believe someone killed the oracle witch," Finn said as she sidled over to me. "I spoke to Mom this morning to see if there's been any buzz in the fairy community, and she said the only talk is that of fear. If it's a fairy, no one is talking."

I conjured up a machete in case I needed it to cut through the vines as we headed toward the cottage. To my surprise, more of the house was visible than it had been earlier. A lot of the kudzu had withered and died off.

"Does this mean without the magic summoning it to kill," Grant said next to me, "the kudzu will just die?"

I shrugged. "Looks like it. That's one relief, I guess."

Doc cleared his throat as we neared Lolita's place. "I just hope the elements and wild animals haven't done too much damage to the body."

"Let's go around back," Alex said. "That's where Lolita is."

As the five of us rounded the corner, I couldn't help but wonder if Doc was right. Would we find Lolita in worse shape than when we left her? If so, I wasn't sure how I could forgive myself. It was imperative we flee when we did, but that didn't seem fair to Lolita and her body. I shouldn't have worried though. Standing guard in a circle around the body were numerous rabbits, squirrels, raccoons, foxes, beavers, and deer.

"Hello, friends," I said. "Thank you for lending a hand."

"It is our pleasure, Princess," the deer said. *"Black Forest King has alerted us all to what is going on. We are here to help in any way we can."*

"Yeah! Yeah, we can help," the raccoon echoed. *"We're good at spying. We see things. Yes, we do."* He rubbed his tiny paws together and nodded. *"Whatever you need, Princess. Whatever you need."*

I smiled, bent down, and ran my hand over the raccoon's head. "Thank you."

"We only had one incident," the deer said. *"After you left, the kudzu tried to take us out, but we could chew through most of the vines, killing the parts that fell away."*

I nodded. "We believe once the leaves die, the magic dissipates."

"That is what we thought as well," a soft-spoken rabbit said.

I stood and told the others what the animals had said.

"Did they notice anyone around?" Alex asked.

"Yes," the deer said. *"While we were eating away at the kudzu, I sent a blue jay to fly overhead and see what he could see. He came back minutes later, telling me there was a woman in a long black cloak by the Douglas fir watching us attack. Sometimes she would whisper under her breath and move her arms. The blue jay could not tell what kind of supernatural she was."*

"Excellent!" I turned to the others. "They saw a woman in a long black cloak. Still not sure if it's a witch or fairy, but at least we know we're looking for a woman."

"Chances are she saw us discover the body," Alex said.

I nodded. "That's probably why the kudzu attacked us when it did."

"Let's get to work," Alex said. "There's got to be a clue here somewhere."

14

W e didn't find a smoking gun telling us who the woman yielding the deadly magic was, but we were able to recover Lolita's body. The only evidence found was the same thing we'd found at the other crime scene—gooey acid-like substance on Lolita's face and neck.

"I'll start the autopsy when I get back to my lab," Doc said. "Unless I find anything significant that requires you to come in, I'll just call and let you know what I found. I assume it will be the same as with Selma."

"And I'll log in the acid substance when we get back to the lab," Finn said, "but other than that, I really didn't find anything new."

"We know we're looking for woman," I said a while later as Alex followed behind Grant's and Doc's vehicles. "Powerful witch or fairy."

"It's still not much to go on," Needles said. *"I mean, there's been lots of witches and fairy families on this island over the last*

four hundred years who probably are holding a grudge for something."

"We'll find it," I said. "GiGi, Mom, and Aunt Starla should be doing their vision spell and preparing to pour over the dozens of leather-bound books the witch coven has in its possession. Something will give."

"Where does that leave us with our suspects?" Alex mused. "They are both men. Think one of them could have hired a woman to do this?"

I shrugged. "It's possible. But I can't really see Flowerbaum doing that. I mean, he seems like the kind of guy who'd have no problem getting his hands dirty if he needed to."

"That was my thought as well," Alex said. "I'd hate to think we've been chasing our tails the last two days."

"Literally for you, Gargoyle. Since your species have tails and all." Needles laughed and laughed, his wings glowing green and yellow.

"Not funny," Alex growled.

I glanced at my watch. "It's nearly time for school to let out. Let's just go back to my place and call it a day. Zoie should be there shortly. Is she flying or driving out?"

"Driving. She wanted to go by the grocery store and pick up some last-minute things for tonight."

I groaned. "This could be one odd dinner."

"I hope she remembers I like salt and caramel together," Needles said from the backseat.

"Not to worry," Alex said. "I saw maple-dipped bacon on her menu."

"Yum!"

15

"I have a fairy by the name of Theodore Leafland," Serena said, looking up from the giant leather-bound book in her hands. "He vowed revenge on the original coven back in 1690 because he felt the coven convinced his betrothed witch, Seraphina Hemlock, to call off the wedding and instead marry a different fairy by the name of Percy Woodman. Leafland swore vengeance on Percy, Seraphina, and the coven. He killed Percy and was harming Seraphina when the witches captured him. Leafland was put to death two days later. Before he died, he vowed his siblings' descendants would avenge his death."

"I guess it could be a female fairy descendent," Alex said, adding another log to the library's fireplace. "Do we know who she might be?"

"There are a couple Leaflands still around the island," GiGi said. "I could make some calls for you."

"That would help," Alex said, sitting down next to me on the chaise lounge.

After a uniquely tasty dinner of fruit loop pancakes, caramelized maple bacon, and peanut butter fried egg sandwiches, Serena, Grant, Mom, GiGi, Aunt Starla, Alex, Zoie, and I had retired to the library to see what we could discover in the old coven books.

"I might have something," Mom said.

"What?" I asked.

"Barisha Flame. In 1763, she was kicked out of the original coven for practicing dark magic. She and her daughter continued to live on the island even though Barisha was shunned by the other witches. Her daughter eventually married a vampire, but Barisha remained a recluse. She died ten years after banishment, and when they found Barisha's body in her cottage, her spell book was opened to a death-curse haunting." Mom looked up from her book. "I guess enough witches felt the death-curse haunting was a threat and added it in the book."

"Barisha Flame," GiGi mused. "Yes, I believe there is a thrice-great granddaughter and quite a few great-great nephews and nieces still around."

I groaned. "Now we have more suspects than we know what to do with."

"I have a question," Zoie said. "You said the oracle witch, Lolita, wrote in the journal that GiGi was next, and to look to the past. What if she meant *GiGi's* past and not the island's past?"

I blinked in surprised at that. GiGi's past had never entered my mind. Mainly because I didn't think she had a sordid past.

"That's actually brilliant," Serena said. "We just *assumed* the oracle meant the island's past."

"Well?" I demanded. "What about your past, GiGi? Anyone you know want to hurt you?"

GiGi scowled. "Of course not! Don't you think I'd remember

if I pissed someone off enough to want to kill not only me, but my friends?"

Mom laid a hand on GiGi's arm. "Your past, Mom. That could be from birth until now. I don't think it's recent. What about when you were a child? Can you think of anything?"

GiGi closed her eyes, then shook her head. "No. I can't think of anything. Being a descendant of one of the original families on the island had its perks as a young witch, and there was some jealousy, but nothing jumps out at me."

"Teenage years?" Alex asked.

GiGi opened her eyes and scoffed. "No. My teenage years were typical. I only..." Her voice trailed off. "Wait. Maybe. I can't believe I forgot about this!"

"What did you remember?" Grant asked.

"The summer of my sixteenth year, me and three other witches were being accepted into the coven during the Coming of Age ceremony—Selma Craftsman, Gretchen Madgical, Claire Thyme, and me. It was a big deal, and we were all excited. Gretchen's strength was animation." GiGi smiled. "I remember once when we were probably ten, she made raindrops dance in the air. Anyway, on the night before the Coming of Age ceremony, a local werewolf farmer was attacked by a mass of vines. He said he was in the barn when the door burst open and these vines came barreling toward him. He shifted and ripped the vines apart with his claws, but not before the vines got some of his livestock. When the coven found out what had happened, they called for the four of us. They demanded to know which one of us had used such deadly magic. All of us denied it, of course."

"Did you know?" Zoie asked.

GiGi shrugged. "I suspected. Anyway, when none of us would admit to it, the older witches got angry. Next thing I knew,

Gretchen stepped forward, crying, saying she saw me in the woods bringing plants to life. I must be the culprit."

"What did you do?" I asked.

"I panicked. I immediately denied it and placed the blame back on Gretchen. By this time, the senior witches were furious and threatening to cancel the Coming of Age ceremony. Just when things were heating up, Lolita came forward and announced she'd had a vision earlier, and she knew the truth. Lolita said she would give the responsible witch one more chance to come forward and do the right thing. When Gretchen remained silent, the oracle told what she knew. In the end, Gretchen was denied acceptance into the coven that year, and her family was disgraced. It ended up they moved from the island less than a year later."

"Then what happened?" Zoie asked.

GiGi shrugged. "I never heard from her or her family again. That was nearly seventy years ago."

I stood and paced in front of the fireplace. "What are we saying? This Gretchen witch has come back to the island *now* to exact her revenge?"

"I'd say that's exactly what's going on," Alex said.

"But why?" GiGi asked. "It wasn't that big of a deal. I mean, yes, she was humiliated and her family left the island, but that's not a reason to murder nearly a century later."

"I've known murder to happen for less," Alex said.

"But why kill Selma?" GiGi asked. "She didn't do anything wrong. Gretchen blamed *me*, not Selma."

"Selma was probably just an easy target," Grant said. "A way to hurt you."

GiGi covered her eyes with her hand. "I can't believe this. I mean, I never put these pieces together. I didn't see it."

"Of course you didn't see it," Mom said gently. "How could you? It happened nearly seventy years ago."

GiGi sighed and lifted her head. "The vines and hybrid plant should have been a clue. A big clue. But it honestly escaped me."

"We need to find out if Gretchen Madgical is on the island," Alex said, "when she arrived, and where she's staying."

"I'll call Lucas right now," Grant said.

Lucas Black, panther shifter, was the island's only pilot.

"What about the other witch in your group?" Zoie asked. "Does Claire Thyme still live on the island? Should someone warn her?"

"As far as I know," GiGi said, "Claire lives on the northwest side of the island. She married a selkie, Noland Waterly, when she was in her early twenties, had a couple kids, and spends her days being a fishmonger's wife. She's not active in our coven, but that's by her own choice."

I stood and poured a glass of wine from the decanter. "At least we are finally putting the pieces together."

Grant strode back into the room. "I put in a call to Lucas to see about recent flights to the island, but his wife said he wasn't due back until tomorrow mid-morning. He had to fly to Phantom Holler, Tennessee for business."

"We'll contact him in the morning then," Alex said.

Grant rubbed his hand down Serena's back. "I'll do a background check on Gretchen Madgical first thing in the morning as well."

I sat back down on the chaise. "Good. Then Alex and I will go pay Claire a visit in the morning."

"Shouldn't I go see her?" GiGi asked.

"No," Alex said. "It's best if you stay away from her. We believe Gretchen has been on the island for two weeks now. At least, that's when Shayla first started tracking this hybrid plant.

Gretchen is learning your routine, GiGi. Right now, Claire isn't a part of your life, so don't make her one."

GiGi nodded. "Makes sense."

"I'll call Deputy Sparks right now," Alex said, "and make sure he drives by Claire's house tonight a couple times. Better to be safe than sorry."

16

Claire Waterly's house was typical of the seaside houses on the northwest side of the island—small, colorful, and smashed together.

I rang the doorbell, and a few seconds later I heard a warbled voice yell out for us to hold on. The woman who opened the door barely reached my chest and was dressed in black slacks, purple sweater, and a full-body apron. Her short, curly hair was neatly combed, and her smile was genuine as she looked out at us behind her oval glasses.

"Hello." Her eyes finally took in our uniforms. "Oh, my." She rested her small hands against her chest. "Is something wrong? Has something happened?"

"Notice how people always have that reaction when they see you, Gargoyle?" Needles quipped.

"No, Mrs. Waterly," Alex said, ignoring Needles' barb. "There's no reason to worry. I'm Sheriff Stone, and this is Agent Shayla Loci."

"Oh, yes. I know who you are, Shayla. Your grandmother and

I used to know each other when we were kids." She dropped her hands. "My, look how you've grown. I'd never have recognized you. Well, what can I do for you both today?"

"Could we come in for a minute?" Alex asked.

Claire furrowed her brow. "Of course. But you said nothing was wrong? My husband, daughter, grandkids, and great-grandkids are all okay?"

"Yes, ma'am." Alex stepped inside, and I followed behind him, shutting the door.

"Come on back to the kitchen. I was in the middle of making cookies for the great-grandkids. I'm the designated babysitter after school until their parents can pick them up after work." She gave me a wink and motioned for us to sit at the kitchen table. "I like to spoil them with cookies after a hard day at school."

"Sounds nice," I said.

"Would you like some milk and cookies?" she asked.

"Yes! Yes, I would." Needles' wings glowed purple as he did a somersault in the air.

I smiled and shook my head. "No, thanks. Sheriff Stone and I just need to ask you some questions."

Claire chuckled. "You may not, but something tells me your porcupine does." Claire handed Needles a cookie, then pulled a chair out from the table and sat down next to me. "Now, what's all this about?"

"Have you heard about Selma Craftsman?" I asked.

Claire's chin trembled, and she pressed her lips together. "I have. It's been years and years since I spoke to Selma, but we would see each other in town every now and again. I just hate someone killed her."

"That's not all." Alex rested his hands on the table. "Yesterday, Lolita Herbton was also murdered."

Claire gasped. "What? I hadn't heard about her." She shook

her head and frowned. "Is there a connection? I wasn't aware the two witches were close."

"They aren't from what GiGi told me," I said.

"Tell her the cookie was delicious," Needles said as he settled onto my shoulder. *"Think I'll just nap right here."*

"Lolita Herbton was years older than us," Claire said. "Probably a good fifteen to twenty years, if I had to guess."

"Needles wants me to tell you the cookie was delicious," I said.

Claire smiled. "Thank you. My great-grandkids love that cookie as well. Gobble them right up."

I leaned forward and rested my arms on the table. "When Sheriff Stone and I found Lolita, we also found a journal. She'd written inside that GiGi was next and that we should look to the past."

Again Claire gasped. "What is going on? Are you saying someone on the island is targeting witches?"

I shook my head. "We think someone on the island is targeting *specific* witches. GiGi told us last night about what Gretchen Madgical did when you guys were sixteen."

Claire cocked her head and frowned. "You think Gretchen Madgical is behind the killings? But she has to be—well, my age. You really think an eighty-something-year-old witch is running around the island killing other witches?"

I shrugged. "It's the best theory we have right now."

Claire ran her hands down her apron. "I wasn't aware Gretchen moved back to Enchanted Island."

"We don't believe she has," Alex said. "We think she may have just arrived a couple weeks ago."

Claire nodded. "And you came here today to warn me? Is that right?"

"Yes," I agreed. "GiGi said you don't attend coven meetings

and aren't active in any witch circles, but we still felt we should warn you."

"Is my family in trouble?" Claire demanded. "Should I tell them what's going on?"

Alex shook his head. "I'm going to put Deputy Sparks on your place for the next day or two until we solve this case. In the meantime, if you see someone hanging around you don't recognize, don't hesitate to call the sheriff's office and let someone know. I'll leave my card with you as well."

"Trust me, I'll keep my family so close they'll beg to go to the bathroom just for some private time."

I smiled. "Good."

* * *

The Enchanted Island airstrip was on the southwest side of the island. The hangar was large and modern, and when Alex pulled to a stop outside the metal building, I could see Lucas Black inside tinkering with his plane. When he saw us, he straightened, wiped his hands on a rag, and met us at the open bay.

"Good morning," Lucas said.

"Morning, Lucas," Alex said. "We don't want to hold you up. We just need to ask you a few questions."

"Wife said you were looking for me. What's up?"

"In the last two weeks, have you flown a female witch to the island? Say maybe mid-eighties?"

Lucas frowned and shook his head. "Can't say I have. Do you know her name?"

"Gretchen Madgical," Alex said.

"Doesn't ring a bell." He motioned for us to follow him through a doorway and into his office. "Let me look over my log." He picked up a clipboard off his desk. "Last two weeks? Nope. No Gretchen Madgical. It was pretty busy around Valentine's Day, flying couples on and off the island." He ran his finger down the page. "I only have two females who were traveling alone—Sonja Howlson and Darbie Forester."

"Forester," I said. "Fairy."

"I think I remember her," Lucas said. "Mainly because she *didn't* speak. I tried engaging her in conversation a couple times on our flight over, but she made it clear she wasn't interested in small talk."

I stuffed my hands in my pockets. "About how old would you say she was?"

Lucas shrugged. "Dunno. Maybe mid-fifties? Hard to say."

We thanked Lucas and strode out of the office and through the hangar.

"Could Gretchen have a daughter?" I mused.

"That's what I'm thinking," Alex said. "I'll text Grant and tell him to run Darbie Forester and see what we get. Since he's already running Gretchen's name, he may already have Darbie on his radar."

I stopped and smacked my forehead.

"I could have done that for you, Princess."

"Haha, Needles." I spun around and called out to Lucas. "Did someone pick up Darbie?"

Lucas shook his head and sauntered over to us. "Nope. She asked if she could rent a car."

I grinned. "So she's driving one of yours?"

"Sure is."

I knew what that meant—we were looking for a tiny camouflaged car. "The Tea for Two car?"

"Yes, ma'am."

The Tea for Two vehicle was eight feet long, had two narrow

seats, and was one of the smallest cars I'd ever seen outside of the Princess Lolly.

"No wonder we haven't been able to spot her," Alex said as he closed the Blazer's door. "In that car she's able to go most places regular cars or SUVs can't."

I nodded. "But we're closing in."

❧ 17 ❧

Opal Earthly-Caraway barely looked up from her computer as Alex and I hurried inside the sheriff's station. The octogenarian witch was a contrast to her twin sister, Pearl, who ran the forensic offices downstairs. Whereas Pearl hated computers or technology of any kind, Opal embraced the modern age.

"I got some relevant information," Grant said from his desk. "I just made fresh coffee if you want some."

I quickly poured Alex and me coffee, tossed Needles a bag of pretzels, then went to sit down next to Grant's desk.

"We aren't looking for Gretchen Madgical," Grant said. "According to the background report, Gretchen Madgical died four weeks ago."

My mouth dropped, and I set my mug down on Grant's desk. "You're kidding?"

"I'm not," Grant said. "Cause of death was heart attack. But you two were on the right track. Gretchen had one daughter,

Darbie Lee Forester. Father is John Forester, fairy. Looks like Gretchen and John were married for less than three years before John left and moved to Ghost Pines. Gretchen and Darbie both lived in Haunted Springs for about fifty years." Grant picked up another piece of paper. "Darbie Forester is fifty-five, single, and self-employed as an herbalist. Yearly income is paltry, and so she lives—or lived—with her mother. No arrests or warrants in either the supernatural or human courts. Never married, and no kids." He wiggled his mouse pad until his computer screen came on. "Here's Darbie's picture."

I stared at the woman on the screen. She seemed older than her fifty-five years—odd for a witch who could probably do a simple glamour. Her short, curly black hair framed a square, weathered face full of wrinkles and sorrow. Her brows were heavy and dark, and her eyes looked like they'd seen a lot. There wasn't a hint of a smile on her driver's license.

Alex took a sip of his coffee. "So Gretchen's death is the catalyst that sent Darbie over the edge?"

I frowned. "So the theory is, the minute her mom died, Darbie exacted revenge on those who supposedly wronged her mother?"

"Seems fitting," Alex said.

Grant tapped his pencil on his desk. "You think Gretchen talked about what happened when she was a teenager to her daughter?"

Alex nodded. "I do. If Gretchen was as enraged as GiGi said, then yes. Those types of sociopaths need an audience. Need someone to hear how they were vilified, and how someone must avenge them. What do you want to bet Darbie grew up listening to her bitter Mom talk incessantly about how she was wrongly accused? How she lost everything because of GiGi. I'm sure when Gretchen finally died, Darbie just automatically took up that mantle for her mom. By killing GiGi and the other witches involved, she could give Gretchen the peace she never had. Or, at least, that's what Darbie believes."

I shuddered. "Sick."

"You're telling me." Needles landed on my shoulder. *"Darbie has to be one sick, twisted lady to use plants to do her killing."*

"I put a hit out for credit cards," Opal said from her desk. "Nothing. No activity for three weeks. If she's staying on the island, she's paying with cash. That includes all her meals and everything else. All cash. I have a call into all the local hotels— The Spellmoore, Traveler's Bay Inn, The Mystic Motel, and Hotel Haunts. If she's on the island, we'll find her."

I reached up and grabbed a pretzel out of Needles' paw. "I need something crunchy. I'll call GiGi and see where the old family homestead was when Gretchen's family lived on the island."

"Get your own pretzels, Princess." Needles flew to the top of a gun rack, his wings glowing red. *"You ain't the only one needing crunch with all this murder talk."*

Smiling, I dug out my cell phone and called GiGi.

"Well?" GiGi demanded. "Is it Gretchen? Have you found her yet?"

"It's not Gretchen Madgical," I said. "She died about a month ago. We think it's her daughter."

GiGi grunted. "Poisoned her daughter's mind, did she? Can't say I'm surprised. So the daughter can animate like her mom?"

"I'd say so," I said. "Looks like her dad was a fairy. So I'd say animating plants would be something she could do."

"Shame on that family," GiGi said. "They should know better than to summon something against its will."

"I know. But don't worry, we're gonna find her." I cleared

my throat. "I called to see if you remember where Gretchen's family lived? Is the house still standing?"

"If memory serves, they lived on the southeast side of the island by the old rock quarry. There was a gravel road about a mile past the quarry on the left. Take it and you should come across the house. Can't say if anyone lives there now."

"Thanks." I frowned when I heard the tell-tell smack of GiGi's lips. "What are you doing?"

"Putting on lipstick."

"Why?"

"Getting ready for my lunch date. I'm meeting Byron at one at the Enchanted Island Café."

"You can't go anywhere alone!" I cried, putting her on speakerphone. "You're in danger."

"I ain't gonna be alone," GiGi said. "I'm gonna be with Byron."

I sighed. "Fine. Then you're going straight back to Mom's after lunch, right?"

"Nope. Gotta run out to my cottage to pick up some things."

"How are you going to get to your cottage?" I asked.

"Gonna drive the Princess Lolly."

Alex cursed. "She doesn't have a license yet!"

"I hear you, Gargoyle," GiGi grumbled. "I think I can manage to take that ridiculous car across the island without incident."

I sighed. "Don't drive. I'll take you."

"Don't be silly," GiGi scoffed. "The Lolly is warded, remember? I'll be fine."

"That's not the point," I argued.

"My ward will hold, Shayla."

Without another word, GiGi disconnected.

"Did she just hang up on me?" I mused.

"She's a stubborn one," Grant said.

I pinched my lips together in anger. "Well, her stubbornness may end up getting her killed."

18

I tried to put GiGi's plans out of my mind, but I just couldn't let it go. As Alex drove toward the rock quarry, I called Mom to get her opinion on GiGi's recklessness.

"I'm trying to talk some sense into her," Mom said.

"See that you do," I said wearily. "Today is going to be hard enough trying to find Darbie without having to chase down GiGi as she joyrides across the island in a lollipop car that could double as a bullseye. Warded or not, she'd be a sitting duck." I disconnected and closed my eyes. "I love GiGi, but sometimes she makes life difficult."

Needles snorted. *"Having known GiGi longer than you, Princess, I can assure you GiGi always makes life more difficult."*

I sighed. "I just don't want her to get hurt. It's like she thinks she's invincible."

Alex turned left after the rock quarry and drove slowly over the loose gravel. The wind had picked up, causing the trees flanking the road to bend and sway.

"Looks like a mailbox on the right," I said. "Think this is the house?"

"Not much else out here," Alex said.

I read the name S. Nightman on the side of the mailbox as Alex turned onto the weeded path leading to the front door of a tiny, rundown cottage. The grass was so tall, I almost missed the For Sale sign staked in the yard.

"Can't tell where the forest ends and the yard begins," Needles joked.

"You coming in or staying out here?" I asked.

"This one could be interesting," Needles said. *"Think I'll join you inside."*

I tripped over a cobblestone paver hidden in the grass and cursed. "If I broke a toe, I'm gonna be mad."

Alex grinned. "Either S. Nightman doesn't have a mower, or he or she is too old to keep up with the lawn care."

It didn't take long to get our answer.

I knocked on the door and seconds later it was opened by an elderly female vampire. Her frail hand lifted in a greeting, and she smiled a toothless grin at us—well, toothless except for her two protruding fangs.

"I'm out," Needles said. *"I'll wait for you by the Blazer."*

I chuckled as he flew from my shoulder.

"Hello, dearies. I wasn't expecting company." Her words were slow and methodical as she stepped back and motioned us inside. "Did you want to look at the house? It's been a good house for me and my husband all these years. I'm Sara. Sara Nightman."

"How long have you lived here?" Alex asked, as I glanced around the empty room with half-packed boxes scattered over the living room.

"Long time. My Arnie bought it from a witch family right

after he sold his barber shop and retired. I guess it's been about seventy years now."

I added up the numbers in my head and blinked in surprise. "Retirement? So that makes you…"

"Old." Sara Nightman slapped her hand against her leg, and I winced. I was afraid her leg might snap in two. "I'm gonna be a hundred forty in two months."

"Is Arnie here?" Alex asked.

Sara shook her head slowly. "Goodness, no. Not for about twenty-six years now. Died while picking beans in our garden."

"I'm sorry," I said.

"Don't be." Sara turned and slowly shuffled toward a wooden chair. "Arnie loved that garden. That's why I dug a hole and buried him right there."

My eyes jerked to Alex. "It's a good thing Needles didn't hear that."

"What's that, dearie?" Sara plopped down in the chair. "I hope you don't mind me sitting? My hips aren't what they used to be." She waved her hand in the air. "You go on and look around. It's a lovely home for a new couple starting out." She gave us another toothless grin. "You two can fill it up with lots of babies."

"Are you moving?" I asked quickly, not wanting to think about the baby comment.

"It's time. My sister has talked me into moving to Garden Pastures. It's that retirement home near the north side of the island. You know it?"

"I do," I said. "I hear it's a nice place."

Sara Nightman frowned. "Do I know you, dearie? Who are your people?"

I smiled and walked closer to her. "GiGi is my grandma."

"Yes. Yes. I knew her mother—your great-grandma."

I crouched down next to her chair. "We're here to ask you if you've seen anyone hanging around lately? Maybe someone you didn't recognize?"

"Can't say I have. But then again, I don't see like I used to. Which is saying something, seeing as how I'm a vampire." Sara's laugh turned into a wheeze, which turned into a cough.

"Can I get you a drink, Mrs. Nightman?" Alex asked.

She waved her hand slowly in the air. "No, young man. I'm fine. Thank you."

"So nothing unusual?" I prompted.

Sara Nightman frowned. "Well, Cupcake has been acting a little strange. Barking at every little thing. Wind blows, Cupcake's barking. She just started that nonsense."

"Who's Cupcake?" I asked.

"My adorable little puppy. She's out back."

"Do you mind if we take a look around the property?" Alex asked.

"Go right ahead." She sighed. "I'm trying to get up the energy to pack the last of my things. This is all I have left to pack except for a plate and a glass and a set of silverware. That sort of thing."

"Let me help you." I waved my hands in the air and levitated the last of the items off the floor and gently placed them in the boxes.

Sara clapped her hands enthusiastically. "Bravo! Thank you so much. Always pays to know a witch."

I grinned. "It sure does. We'll just go outside and look around now."

Needles was sunning himself on the top of the Blazer when we walked outside.

"We're going around back," I said. "Seems Cupcake has been barking a lot lately."

Needles perked up. *"Cupcake? That's a cute name. Bet it's a cute little dog. I'll come with."*

The three of us had just turned the corner to the back of the house when a loud, deep bark permeated the air. Standing in the middle of the backyard was a massive brown and black English Mastiff...with a pink bow around its neck.

"*You're* Cupcake?" I asked incredulously.

Needles did a somersault in the air, laughing hysterically, his wings glowing green and yellow.

"Stop it!" I hissed at Needles.

"Careful," Alex said. "Cupcake may decide you're a treat and gobble you right up."

Needles straightened and flew back to my shoulder.

"It's okay," Cupcake said, the gravely grit of his voice tinged with resignation. *"I've heard it all, Princess. My mistress means well, but she doesn't have a good grasp on reality."*

I couldn't help my grin. "I don't have to tell you you're not what we were expecting. Cupcake brings up images of..."

"A cute little fluffy girl dog?" He shook his head, causing the pink bow to twist around his neck. *"Like I said, I get that a lot."*

I cleared my throat. "Can you tell me if you've noticed anything suspicious the last few days? Mrs. Nightman says you've been barking more than usual."

"My mistress doesn't see well anymore, so she's not aware of what's really going on."

"And what's that?" I asked.

"I'm not sure, but it feels like someone is here, and I am scared for my mistress." He bared his teeth and growled. *"I can show you where I get the bad feeling."*

Alex and I trudged after Cupcake through the backyard until we came to the edge of the forest.

"Through there. I don't dare go any farther. If something

98

were to happen to me, my mistress would have no one to look after her. So I stay outside in the backyard and do my best to guard her."

"But you feel something here?" I prodded.

"Yes. A darkness I can't explain. Like something bad is watching and waiting."

Cupcake turned and ambled back toward the cottage, and Needles flew from my shoulder and whipped out two of his razor-sharp quills.

"You guys take the right," Alex said, "and I'll take the left."

Needles and I had barely walked ten yards before I saw the broken twigs and footprints on the ground. Someone had definitely been here recently.

"I think I found something," Alex called out.

Needles and I hurried over to where he stood.

"It's totally out of place," Alex said.

I levitated the small, crushed flower and nodded. "Yep. It's sea lavender. I remember seeing some—let's see, where was I? Down on the south side of the island near the water about three miles from High Seas Bar & Grill. It wasn't in the same location where I first stumbled over the drag marks a few weeks ago, but it's not too far from there. Do you think that's where Darbie is hiding out?"

Alex nodded. "I think we definitely have a good place to start."

19

"Do me a favor?" I said as Alex crossed into town. "Drop me off at the bakery so I can pick up my vehicle. I'll follow GiGi to her cottage, then we can meet up at High Seas Bar & Grill and scope the area an acre at a time."

It was almost two o'clock when Alex dropped me off, which meant the bakery would close in another hour. Heading inside, I waved to Serena and Tamara behind the counter, then made small talk with the few customers inside the store before heading to the display case.

"We have some cookies that need to go today," Tamara said. "You want to take some home with you?"

I grinned. "Do I? Heck, yeah."

Tamara laughed and boxed up a dozen assorted cookies.

"You heading home now?" Serena asked.

"No. GiGi is being difficult." I quickly filled them in on her foolish plan to go back to her cottage for a while after she had lunch with Byron. "So I thought I'd drive her out to her place."

"I have an idea," Serena said. "How about I ride with GiGi to her cottage, and then I ride with you back to town? GiGi has a baby box for me. According to her, she's been knitting these items for about five years now, hoping one of us would eventually need them."

I grinned. "Sounds like GiGi. That would be a great idea, but I'm only going as far as High Seas Bar & Grill. Alex and I need to sweep that area for clues."

"Even better," Serena said. "I've been so hungry lately it's ridiculous. I'll call Grant and have him meet me at the High Seas for a between-meals snack." Serena turned to Tamara. "Would you mind if I cut out a little early?"

Tamara waved her hand in the air. "Go! I'll clean up here. Afterward, I'm going to go pick up Baby Jayden from Zac's aunt's house and keep her until he gets off work around eight tonight."

Serena gave Tamara a quick hug. "If I see Zac tending bar at High Seas, I'll tell him you said hi."

I grinned and locked arms with Serena. "Let's go see if GiGi is still on this hot date of hers."

"How fun," Needles grumbled. *"A geriatric stakeout."*

We walked across the street and down the sidewalk until we hit the café. I was about to pull open the glass door when GiGi and Byron strolled outside.

"Whaddya all doing here?" GiGi demanded.

"I thought I'd ride with you to your place," Serena said, "and pick up the box you were telling me about."

GiGi scowled. "Don't think I don't know what this is!"

"Hush," I said. "Say goodbye to Byron so we can go."

I jogged back across the street to where my Bronco was parked and waited for GiGi and Serena to cram themselves into the Princess Lolly.

"That has to be the most humiliating car ever made," Needles said as he settled down on the front seat.

"Nope. You haven't seen the camouflage Tea for Two cars Lucas rents out, have you?"

"Can't say I have."

"Trust me, *those* are the most humiliating cars ever made."

I pulled out behind GiGi and settled in to follow her the thirty-five miles back to our secluded houses. We were cruising down the road about seven miles from our turnoff when movement on the side of the road caught my eye. I leaned forward and squinted through the trees to see what had captured my attention —when huge vines emerged from the ditches and crossed both sides of the road in front of GiGi's car, wrapping around her front tires.

I screamed as the Princess Lolly came to an abrupt stop, causing the back end to flip over and land on the car's roof, shattering all the windows. The two lollipops welded to the roof sent sparks flying along the blacktop as the car turned in a slow circle.

Slamming on my brakes—and coming a hair's breadth from plowing into GiGi and Serena—I hopped out of the Bronco and ran to the Princess Lolly.

"GiGi!" I screamed. "Serena! Are you guys okay?"

"Be careful, Princess." Needles zipped ahead of me, his wings glowing black and gray.

"We're okay," GiGi called out. "The ward held up pretty good."

"Could have fooled me," I grumbled.

Digging in my pocket, I yanked out my cell phone and called Alex.

"You need to get here fast," I yelled. "Serena and GiGi were in an accident. I think they're okay, but we're gonna need an ambulance." My breath caught on a sob. "I need to make sure Serena is okay. The baby."

"Where are you?" Alex demanded.

I gave him our location, hung up, then squatted down near the broken back window. "I got help coming. Be careful getting out of your seatbelt, GiGi. Gravity and all."

"Allow me, Princess." Needles flew through the back window and looked around inside. *"You okay, Serena?"*

"I'm okay, Needles. I'd like to stop hanging upside down, but other than that, I think I'm okay."

I rubbed my palms over my face. "The paramedics should be here in—"

I was cut off when Alex landed next to me—Grant in his arms. Any other time, I'd have made a joke about the massive mountain of a werewolf being carried somewhere, but today wasn't the day. One look on his face told me he was terrified and angry.

Grant all but sprang out of Alex's arms, shifted to his werewolf form, then leaped over to Serena's side of the car. Using his supernatural strength, he ripped the door off its hinges, threw it behind him, then shifted back to human.

"You okay, baby?"

Serena burst into tears. "I th-th-think so!" More sobs. "I ju— just want out."

"You got here fast," I said as I watched Grant reach in and help Serena out of her harness.

"After dropping you off at the bakery, I went back to the station to look over some things. Grant and I were both there. Paramedics should be here shortly. As will Weston."

I shook my head and sighed. "I think my family is single-handedly keeping that man in business."

"What about me?" GiGi grumbled. "You two just gonna stand there and watch me hang upside down?"

I shot Alex a grin as Needles flew out of the Lolly and landed on my shoulder.

"I vote yes, Princess." Needles' wings glowed purple, and his little belly shook with laughter. *"Let's leave her inside."*

"I was thinking we should wait for the paramedics," I said.

"By the time they get here," GiGi hollered, "the blood will be in my head, and I'll pass out!"

"Fingers crossed." Needles fell off my shoulder, laughing and turning somersaults. I knew it was relief laughter, so I just grinned and let him ride it out.

As Serena crawled out the passenger-side window into Grant's arms, I hurried over to GiGi's side. "Ya know, a little red in your face is a good color for you."

"Oh, for the sake of the goddess, get me out right now!" GiGi snapped. "If I have to release my own buckle and levitate myself out of here, I'm gonna make sure my next spell is one of hair loss —for all of you!"

Throwing back my head and giving in to the "relief laughter" along with everyone else, I whispered a buoyancy spell that would hold her in place as GiGi undid her buckle. Once she was safely undone, I gently lowered her, and she quickly righted herself in the seat and crawled out the window, careful to avoid the shattered glass.

I heard the siren before I saw the ambulance.

"Who's gonna tell Mom and Aunt Starla?" I asked, helping GiGi up off the ground.

"I already called," Alex said. "Spoke to both of them. They will meet us at the hospital."

"I ain't goin' to no hospital!" GiGi snapped, brushing away my hands. "I'm perfectly fine."

"*You* may be," I said, "but we need to make sure about Serena."

Grief passed over GiGi's face and she nodded. "You're right." GiGi reached up, grabbed my shirt, and yanked me down to eye level. "Anything happens to that baby, and I'll rip Darbie Forester apart with my bare hands."

"Understood."

"By the way," GiGi said. "I was wrong the other day."

I arched an eyebrow. "Oh? About what?"

GiGi grinned and rubbed her head. "Getting in an accident in that ridiculous car isn't exactly like hitting a fluffy cloud. Don't get me wrong, the wards held, but it was still a bumpy ride."

I laughed and gathered GiGi close for a hug. "I'm glad you're okay. I was scared out of my mind when I saw you two flip."

"She's mine," GiGi said. "When you two finally track Darbie down, I want a piece of that witch. You hear me?"

"I hear you, GiGi."

Twenty minutes later, Serena, GiGi, and Grant were inside the ambulance and on their way to the hospital. Weston had the Princess Lolly hooked up to the wrecker, and Alex and I were processing the scene while Needles questioned the local animals.

"Nothing magical about the kudzu now." I yanked the lifeless vines off the front tires and shoved them inside an evidence bag. "A part of me is angry I didn't try and track Darbie down. I mean, I know a locator spell would have been pointless because she's more than likely cloaking herself, but I could have tried to track her."

"That's what Needles is doing now," Alex said. "And your mind was where it should have been—on making sure Serena and GiGi were safe. We'll get her, Shayla. That I can promise you."

I sighed. "I know. I'm just—I don't know. I'm used to the bad guy coming after me, not my family. I'm the one usually getting blown up or shot—not Serena and GiGi. If Darbie had made a play for me and the Bronco, I'd know where to focus my rage. But she didn't. She went after Serena and GiGi."

"And in doing so, she put the final nail in her coffin." He sidled up next to me, gathered me in his arms, and kissed my forehead. "When word gets out what she did to GiGi and Serena, every witch and plenty of other supernaturals on this island will be on the hunt. Darbie has no idea how tight this community can be—especially when you *hurt* one of their own."

We waved as Weston pulled out and headed toward his shop, towing the smashed Lolly behind him.

A horn behind us beeped, and seconds later, Zoie was parked and running. Barreling into both of us, she wrapped her arms around us. "I was in the school parking lot when I got the word." Her voice was muffled against my arm. "Why didn't you guys call me?" She stood back and glared at us. "I was worried sick! I almost flew here, but Brick convinced me to calm down and drive out here. Where's Serena? How is she? How's the baby? What about GiGi? Is she okay?"

Alex gathered his daughter up in his arms and ran his hands over her head and shoulders. "Hush now. Everything is fine. The girls are at the hospital getting looked over."

I glanced over my shoulder and waved to Brick, Zoie's boyfriend, who was standing next to Zoie's smart car. "Why don't you and Brick head to the hospital? I'm sure Mom and Aunt Starla could use the company and the distraction."

Zoie smiled. "Okay. Are you guys heading to the hospital?"

"As soon as we can," Alex said. "We need to finish up here first, then we'll be there."

20

"Anything?" Alex called out to me from somewhere in the forest.

"Nothing yet," I hollered back.

"We're close to the water," Needles said. *"Maybe she's staying near the beach. You said the Venus flytrap has to have constant water."*

"Let's go."

The closer we got to the water's edge and away from the road, the thicker and denser the foliage became. Just when I thought I was going to have to blast my way through, a clearing opened, and Needles and I stumbled out onto the sand. I took a moment to revel in the feel of the salty sea air blowing across my face before taking in my surroundings.

Unlike the other three sides of the island, with their high rocky cliffs, this side of the island had a flatter terrain and low cliffs.

"I'll look around and see what I can find."

"Thanks. I have an idea. I think I know someone who might be able to help us."

"Meet back up in a few, Princess. Be on the lookout and be careful."

As Needles zipped away, I slipped off my shoes and socks and walked down to the water's edge, enjoying the feel of the cool water as it rolled over my feet. Dropping to my knees, I leaned forward and placed my hands in the water, touching my palms to the sand.

I closed my eyes and drew on Dad's power and connection with the island—something I'd recently learned I could do. "Kraken? Can you hear me? It's Shayla Loci, Black Forest King's daughter." I waited a beat and tried again. "I know you prefer the west side of the island, but could you please heed my call? I need your help."

"I hear you Daughter of Black Forest King. I am on my way."

I stayed where I was, eyes closed, palms on the sand and submerged in shallow water. Less than a minute later, I heard a splash and opened my eyes. About ten yards out to sea, Kraken's head appeared above the water.

"What is it you need from me, Shayla Loci?"

"The island is under attack," I said. "A witch is using a hybrid Venus flytrap and welwitschia to kill other witches on the island. I know the Venus flytrap needs excessive water to survive, so I thought maybe you might have seen such a creature roaming near the water's edge."

"I have not. But now that I know, I will keep a watch over the perimeter of the island."

"Thank you. I know it's a lot to ask, given the size of Enchanted Island, but we are desperate."

"I am here to help the island in whatever capacity I can. Your father gave me sanctuary when I was being hunted by sailing ships as they crossed the ocean. I have been here since before there were even inhabitants on the island. I owe Black Forest King an enormous debt."

"If it helps, I think the witch and her hybrid are staying on the south side of the island."

"Then I will patrol this side of the island more than the others. I wish you luck, Daughter of Black Forest King."

When Kraken slipped beneath the water, I lifted my hands from the sand and stood. Brushing off my pants, I turned when I heard Needles yelling my name.

"I found something, Princess!"

"Alex!" I called out. "Can you hear me?"

"I can hear you."

I let out a little scream as I whirled and saw Alex behind me in the distance. "You scared me!"

He chuckled and sauntered over to me. "Sorry. I didn't want to disturb you. Were you speaking with Kraken?"

"Yes. He's going to patrol the south side of the island for us. He said he hasn't seen anything suspicious, but he rarely comes to this side. He will now."

"Good. What did you find?"

"It's me." Needles hurried over to where we stood, his wings glowing red and orange. *"I think I found where Darbie has been hiding."*

We jogged after Needles as he headed for what I thought was the forest—only to come up short when Needles moved tangled vines aside, and a cave entrance emerged.

"Nice work, Needles." I threw up a light orb as Alex and I ducked inside.

Lying next to a fire pit was a yoga mat, travel pillow, and a thin blanket.

"Think she's running?" Alex mused. "Or do you think she'll be back?"

I shrugged. "Can't really say. There's nothing significant left behind."

"But we're close," Needles said, his wings throwing off light around the darkened cave. *"We're definitely nipping at her heels, Princess."*

* * *

The Enchanted Island Hospital wasn't your typical hospital. Instead of over-worked doctors and nurses, harsh medicines, and sterile depressing rooms, our hospital was filled with witches and fairies who specialized in medicine and magic, and the rooms were designed to fit the individual supernatural's need.

"How is she?" I asked as I hurried inside the waiting room, Alex and Needles behind me. "Is the baby okay?"

Mom stood and engulfed me in a hug. "Serena and the baby are fine. The doctor wants to keep her overnight, just to be sure, but they will be fine. The doctor said as soon as Serena gets settled, we can go see her."

Relief flooded my body, and I blinked back the onslaught of tears that filled my eyes. "Good. I didn't want to admit, even to myself, how worried I was."

"We all were," Mom said.

I glanced over at GiGi, who was staring blankly at the wall across the room. "She okay?"

Mom followed my gaze. "She will be. Right now, she's blaming herself."

"Zoie," Alex said, "I want you to fly to Shayla's castle tonight to stay. Do not drive—fly."

Zoie nodded. "I understand."

Grant cleared his throat from the doorway. "Doctor says you all can say goodnight to Serena."

Aunt Starla, Walt Hawkins, and Zoie jumped up from their seats and quickly exited the room. Mom kissed my cheek and followed after them, leaving Grant, GiGi, Alex, Needles, and me alone in the waiting room.

"I know I don't need to tell you this," Grant said between clenched teeth, "but we need to find this witch, no matter what it takes. Right now, I don't care if we have to turn this island upside down. I want her found."

"I know," I whispered.

"We need to come up with a way to draw her out," Alex said.

"I agree," I said. "But how?"

"I think I have a way," GiGi said, standing and sidling over to us. "But I need to talk to Black Forest King."

"We can go now," I said. "Alex can fly me, and Zoie can fly you, GiGi."

Alex's cell phone rang. "It's dispatch." He slid his finger over the green phone and answered. "This is Sheriff Stone." There was a pause as Alex's eyes met mine. "I got it. We'll be right there. Send Deputy Sparks there now. We are about twenty minutes out." He disconnected and shoved the phone back in his pants. "It's Claire Waterly. There's been an attack. Let's go, Shayla. Grant, you stay here with Serena. We'll let you know what's happened."

"Stay with GiGi," I said to Needles. "Don't let her out of your sight. Protect her at all costs."

"I can protect myself," GiGi sniffed.

Ignoring her, I kept my eyes on Needles. "I mean it. Don't let her out of your sight."

Needles pulled two quills from his back, his wings glowing purple and red. *"You have my word, Princess. I will protect the old witch with my life."*

D eputy Sparks, the ambulance, and a firetruck were all parked near the northwest boat dock where months before I'd been shot in the shoulder. A dour-faced man was sitting on a gurney, arguing with the paramedics as Claire Waterly paced in front of him.

"What's going on?" Alex asked.

Claire sagged with relief and hurried over to us. "It's my husband. He was coming in off the boat from work when a giant kelp came out of the water, wrapped around his legs, and dragged him toward the ocean. Luckily, two selkie fishermen were still around and were able to keep him from being dragged out to sea." She shook her head. "And this is where the story gets weird. One of the selkie's *swears* he saw Kraken emerge from under the water, wrap three tentacles around the kelp, and snap it in two, making it let go of Boyd."

I nodded. "Kraken broke the magical connection when he snapped the kelp in two."

"What do you mean?" Claire asked.

I shook my head. "It's not important. What *is* important is that your husband is okay."

Claire sniffed and swiped at her nose. "I can't believe Gretchen tried to kill my husband. Why didn't she go for me?"

"It's actually not Gretchen Madgical," I said. "Gretchen died earlier this month. We believe it's her daughter."

Claire ran her hands through her curly gray hair. "And all this because her mother refused to take responsibility for something that happened nearly seventy years ago?"

"And I'm telling you I'm perfectly fine," Claire's husband snapped from the gurney. "I'm a selkie. I live both in and out of water. Trust me, it'll take more than some damn kelp to take me out of this world. Now, leave me be and let me go home."

"Boyd Alan Waterly," Claire snapped as she turned around and faced her husband, "you hush up and let these nice men take care of you."

Boyd flushed and looked down at the ground. "Yes, ma'am."

Alex and I headed toward the dock, but instead of stepping up onto the platform, we walked under the pier until we stood at the water's edge. I lifted my hand in greeting when I saw Kraken about ten yards off the shore.

Bending down, I touched the brownish-green blob of kelp lying near my feet. "Magic. I can still feel it."

"I did not see the wielder of the magic," Kraken said from his location in the water. *"I am sorry, Daughter of Black Forest King."*

"It's okay. You saved the selkie's life, and that was more important. Alex and I are close to discovering where the witch is hiding."

"Then I wish you luck, Shayla Loci." Kraken slipped beneath the water and was gone.

"Do you want to go see your dad?" Alex asked. "Deputy Sparks can write up the report and process the scene."

I nodded, dug my cell phone out of my pocket, and called GiGi. "You still at the hospital? Good. Have Zoie fly you and Needles to Black Forest. Alex and I are on our way."

22

The fireflies must have known the seriousness of the situation, because when Alex and I crossed into Black Forest a little while later, for the first time ever, they didn't fly up to greet us and ply us with a thousand questions.

As Alex set me down next to GiGi and Zoie, I drew in a deep breath and breathed in the essence of my dad and the forest— giving me a jolt of calmness and healing. It didn't matter if my body was weary from mental or physical fatigue, the forest always somehow sensed my need and healed me quickly.

"I am angered by what could have happened to Serena and her baby," Dad said. *"It is time to put an end to the witch who has dared to come onto my island and hurt those I love most."*

Grinning, I levitated myself the four feet it took for me to be level with dad's trunk thanks to his huge roots. I wrapped my arms around him as best I could and rested my head against his rough bark. "I love you, Dad." Stepping back, I nodded once. "And you're right. It's time Darbie Forester realizes exactly *who* she is messing with."

"Then let me tell you what I have in mind," GiGi said.

Fifteen minutes later, GiGi finally stopped talking.

"I think it sounds like a solid plan," Dad said. *"Assuming Darbie Forester knows nothing of me, where Black Forest is, my powers, and therefore Shayla's true powers."*

"I don't believe she does, Black Forest King," GiGi said. "Let's be honest, most supernaturals who have lived on this island their entire lives don't know what your true powers are, much less Shayla's."

"She's right," I said. "Heck, *I'm* not even sure what all my powers are."

Zoie laughed and looked up from playing with one of the forest rabbits. "It's true."

"Which will work to our advantage," Alex said. "Think about it, most of the stories Darbie grew up on were about GiGi when she was just a teenager, not as a witch in her eighties with a daughter who fell in love with a genius loci and bore a daughter —who in her own right is powerful and magical." He pulled me close to him, and I rested my head on his shoulder. "Darbie does not know the rest of the story. She only has a small, narrow view of her reality."

"And that will be her downfall," Dad said.

"Yes," Alex agreed. "She will underestimate the true power of this family."

"You do not believe Darbie Forester has spoken to other Enchanted Island citizens?" Dad asked. *"Asked around about GiGi?"*

I shook my head. "I don't think so. I think she purposely stayed away from town and from supernaturals in general. That's why it's taken her two weeks to finally act."

"She had to rely on her own reconnaissance mission," Alex said. "And that takes time."

I snorted. "And let's be honest, from what she's seen, I doubt she's too scared."

"What makes you say that?" Dad asked.

Needles dropped down from one of Dad's branches and landed next to Zoie, who was sitting on the ground. *"We haven't exactly been on our game, Black Forest King."*

"Needles is right," I said. "We've given her no reason to fear us. The day we found Lolita in her backyard, and the kudzu attacked us, we didn't exactly stay and fight. Instead, we ran back to the Blazer and hightailed it out of there." I held up a hand when Alex looked like he was going to interrupt me. "Not out of fear, so much as we weren't sure what we were dealing with and needed to get to safety. I think Darbie sees us as weak and inconsequential, and that's why she hasn't really gone after me or Mom very hard. We may be direct descendants of her hatred, but she's dismissed us. She's too focused on GiGi."

"And you are positive Darbie Forester will take the bait?" Dad asked.

"I know she will," GiGi said. "She thinks we're still chasing our tails. She won't suspect a thing." GiGi stood and looked at Black Forest King. "This time tomorrow, Darbie Forester will never have the opportunity to hurt this family or any of the citizens of Enchanted Island again."

"Let's bring her down," I said.

❦ 23 ❦

I t took a lot of convincing, but Alex and I finally got Zoie off to school the next morning. She'd fought valiantly to skip school and spend the day with us rehashing the plan, but in the end, Alex's firm no won out. Not that I could blame Zoie. If I'd been told to go to school and focus on class instead of helping my family, I'd have dug my heels in as well.

But we needed to keep up the appearance this was just another typical day on the island, and in order to do that, Zoie needed to do her part.

"Just stick to the plan," I told Zoie. "After school, drive to Brick's house and leave your car. Fly to Mom's, pick her and Needles up, then fly to Black Forest. Stay there in Black Forest until your dad and Grant get there. GiGi and I will draw Darbie out on our end. Don't deviate, and don't forget to bring the wand I gave you for your birthday that was fashioned from one of Black Forest King's branches. You will need that extra help."

"I won't," Zoie promised.

Once she was gone and on her way to school, Alex, Needles,

and I headed into town to see Mom and GiGi. Mom had oatmeal, scrambled eggs, and bacon on the table when Alex and I ambled into her kitchen. GiGi was already at the table eating.

"I was starving," GiGi said. "Couldn't keep waiting. Gotta eat while it's hot."

Smiling, I leaned down and kissed her cheek. "How did you sleep?"

GiGi shrugged. "Okay. Ready for this to be over."

I sat down next to her and filled my plate while Mom set down a mug of coffee in front of Alex.

"And we're sure this will work?" Mom asked.

"Yes." I set my fork down and wiped my mouth with a napkin. "Drawing her out is the only way. We need Darbie to think our guard is down, so she'll strike."

"Then let's finish up here and get started." Mom handed Needles a piece of bacon off her plate. "The sooner we start, the faster we can bring this crazy witch down."

I chuckled and picked up my fork. "That seems to be the catchphrase going around these last two days."

* * *

Dash Stryker was behind his desk when his secretary escorted Mom, GiGi, Needles, and me back to his office. Standing and smiling, he motioned for us to sit at the table on the far side of the room.

"I'm excited to start on your cottage." He set down a tray with four mugs, myriad tea bags, cubed sugar, and honey. "Water is boiling. It'll just be a second."

Once the tea was poured and doctored, Dash got down to business. "I want you to know I understand the seriousness of this project, and I am honored you chose me. Especially since–well, with what happened with my brother out by your land. I have chosen three other men, besides myself, to head this project. The four of us know the honor and privilege it is to be so close to Black Forest. We will not let you down."

It was odd hearing him say the very thing I had been thinking about on my walk home from GiGi's the other night. We had definitely come full circle.

"With the four of us working out there, I predict we could have your new place finished by mid-April."

Mom gasped. "So quickly? How?"

Dash chuckled. "I have a vampire, two werewolves if you include me, and a witch. That's supernatural speed, strength, endurance, and magic. Trust me, we can get this done for you quickly and get it done right."

Needles did a somersault in the air. *"Black Forest King will be happy to hear this news."*

I smiled. "Guess we should do some shopping for countertops, paint, floors, and all the fun stuff soon."

"I'm absolutely thrilled," Mom said. "Best news I've had in a few days."

Dash winced. "I heard about Selma Craftsman and Lolita Herbton. I'm sorry to hear of their deaths."

GiGi pressed her lips together. "Thank you."

A little while later, we left the construction office and headed to the bakery. It wasn't that we were hungry or thirsty, we just needed something to do, and the bakery was a constant in our daily ritual. So we would go to the bakery and hang out.

I opened the front door for GiGi and Mom to walk through, then halted and gasped. "What are you doing here?"

Serena waved, finished ringing up a customer, then called out to Tamara she was going to take a quick break. Throwing some cookies onto a tray, she walked over to where Aunt Starla sat at a table near the window.

"I've already heard it from Mom," Serena said. "I don't need to hear it from you three."

"Four. I'm not exactly thrilled you're here, either." Needles landed on my shoulder. *"You need to take care of that baby on board."*

"Maybe they can talk some sense into you," Aunt Starla said. "Because obviously I can't."

Serena patted her mom on the shoulder. "I'm not overdoing it. I promise."

"How are you even out of the hospital?" I asked.

Serena waved her hand in the air. "I was released at nine this morning. I'm perfectly healthy." She rested her palms against her stomach. "And the little witchy werewolf is just fine as well. Trust me, I have a feeling this baby is gonna be strong and capable."

I blinked back the sudden onslaught of tears and wondered for the twentieth time why it was I seemed to be so emotional lately. I'd almost burst into tears more times in the last week than I had my whole life. But hearing Serena talk about the baby inside her tugged at my heartstrings. GiGi was right, things were changing, and now we were taking another step into a new chapter of our lives. Our family's legacy would live on, and that thrilled me. Especially knowing I wasn't the sole bearer of that responsibility.

"Is Grant at the sheriff's station?" I asked.

Serena gave me a knowing look and nodded. "Yes." She sat down and leaned forward. "And as upset as I am that I'm going to miss the big showdown, I do understand. I have someone else besides myself to think about now. But I demand to hear everything once it's over."

I laughed. "Deal."

While we stayed at the bakery, nibbled on desserts, and pretended to look busy, I continually scanned the streets outside. Not that I expected Darbie to come this close to town.

"You're anxious, Princess. I can feel it." Needles rested his tiny head against my neck, his wings brushing my shoulder.

I reached over and ran my hand under his chin. "I'm just ready for this to be over."

I'd just finished my third cookie when GiGi stood. "I think it's about time we went back to Serenity's so I can take a nap. Gotta rest up for later."

❧ 24 ❧

At exactly three-thirty, Zoie sent me a text letting me know she was on her way to Brick's house to drop off her car. She would be at Mom's shortly.

"Don't forget," I said for the third time as I hugged her and Mom goodbye, "you stay in your gargoyle form until the fight is over. You understand?"

"Don't worry, Shayla. Sheesh. Between you and Dad, I got it. I promise."

Tears filled my eyes. "I just don't want anything to happen to you. You mean so much to me, and the thought of you getting hurt is—" I broke off as a sob escaped.

"I will guard her with my life, Princess."

Zoie blinked back her own tears. "I understand. Trust me. And you're the one who's going to be in the line of fire more than me. I'm just taking out magical vines. *You* need to take care."

"I will. See you at the castle shortly…I hope."

Once Mom, Needles, and Zoie were in the air and headed

toward Black Forest, I sent Alex a text and told him he needed to get Grant and travel to Black Forest as well.

"That just leaves you and me," I said to GiGi. "Ready?"

"As I'll ever be."

We were about five miles from the turnoff to my castle when I glanced at GiGi and gave her a nod. Understanding, GiGi whispered under her breath, and seconds later, white smoke billowed out from under the hood of my Bronco.

"Stop!" I cried. "Look up ahead."

GiGi released the spell and snorted. "Did that sneaky witch have the same idea as us?"

"Looks like it. Guess it won't be us breaking down hoping for a ride. We'll be picking her up."

"Fine, but we aren't letting the flesh-eating plant or killer vines inside. That's where I draw the line."

I slowed the Bronco down to scan the surrounding area. No sign of either around. "You think she's stashed them near our place?"

GiGi scowled. "If she ruins our plan, I'm gonna be mad."

"Something tells me if she knew about the others in Black Forest waiting to pounce, she wouldn't be pulling this desperate act."

GiGi laughed. "The same desperate act we were about to pull?"

I grinned. "Something like that. Okay, let's play it her way. You ready?"

"Bring it."

When we were about twenty feet from the ridiculously tiny car, I pulled my Bronco to the side of the road, and GiGi and I hopped out.

"Hello." I gave her what I hoped was a friendly smile. "Looks like you could use some help." GiGi and I stopped near the hood of her car. "I'll admit I don't know much about cars, but my house isn't that far away. I could give you a lift to my place so you can call Weston Tow Truck. He's the best."

GiGi snorted. "He's the *only* towing company on the island."

Darbie closed the hood of her car. "I noticed I have no cell signal along this stretch of highway."

I nodded. "There's about a three-mile gap where the trees make it impossible to get signal. But like I said, I can take you to my house. I have a phone you can use."

Darbie pressed a fingertip to her lips, trying to look as though she wasn't sure what to do. It was all I could do not to roll my eyes.

"As you can see," I said, pointing to my uniform, "I'm with law enforcement in a way. I'm the island's game warden. This is my grandma, GiGi. She's lived here her whole life."

"GiGi?" Darbie mused. "An unusual name."

GiGi smiled tightly. "My given name is Matilda, but everyone on the island calls me GiGi."

"I know this car," I said. "Lucas Black owns them and lets vacationers drive them. Are you visiting Enchanted Island, then?"

The woman rested a hand against her chest. "Oh, yes. Dear me. Did I not introduce myself? My name is Darbie Forester. I'm from a small supernatural town I'm sure you've never heard of. And you are?"

"Shayla Loci."

Darbie smiled. "Well, now that we've been properly introduced, I guess there's no reason why I can't take you up on your generous offer for help." She bit her lip and looked questioningly at me. "Do you think my vehicle will be safe here?"

"It will."

I motioned for GiGi and Darbie to go in front of me. No way

was I turning my back on the devious woman. Plus, I wanted to keep an eye out for any wayward kudzu or a flesh-eating Venus flytrap roaming about.

Once we were inside the Bronco, I pulled out onto the road and headed toward the castle, doing my best not to stare at Darbie through my rear-view mirror. I didn't want to make her suspicious.

"Our turnoff is coming up on the left," I said.

"This seems like a remote location," Darbie said. "I don't believe I've seen another house for miles."

"And you won't." I turned left at the road. "From this turnoff up until you reach our house some five miles north, it's just me and GiGi."

"The isolation doesn't bother you?" Darbie asked.

"Not in the least," GiGi said. "No one would dare step foot out here."

I didn't miss the smug smile that slid over Darbie's face. "Is that so? Well, how fortunate for you."

There was an awkward silence for another mile or two before GiGi's cottage came into view.

"I take it one of you lives here?" Darbie asked.

"GiGi does," I said, "but we'll have to go another mile up the road to my home. GiGi doesn't have a landline."

We passed GiGi's cottage and bumped along the half-gravel/half-weeded road until my imposing stone castle came into view. Knowing everyone was hiding and ready to attack made my gut clench in anticipation.

"What a lovely home," Darbie said. "So unexpected."

I parked in the gravel driveway and waited as GiGi and Darbie exited the Bronco. I quickly scanned the area, but I didn't see a visual of Darbie's magical plants *or* a visual of my posse.

"My phone is inside," I said, just a tad bit louder than necessary.

"Oh, this is lovely." Darbie stopped in the middle of my yard. "I could stand here all day and look at the trees. How lucky you are to live in such a beautiful home on an even lovelier property. My mother would have loved seeing this."

The hairs on the back of my neck stood up. This was it. "Oh, is your mother not with you visiting the island?"

"No."

The coldness in her voice had my witchy senses tingling. "Well, if you'd like to—"

"My mother died a few weeks ago," Darbie continued, as though I hadn't spoken. "Died from grief, humiliation, and bitterness." Her eyes flashed to GiGi. "All because of *you*!"

"Me?" GiGi pressed a hand to her chest and blinked her eyes innocently. "Whatever did I do? I've never met you before in my life."

"But you knew my mother!" Darbie all but screamed. "It's because of *you* my mother doesn't live on this beautiful island. Because of *you* she never had the chance to have something as wonderful as all this! Because of *you* and your *lies*!"

I heard the low buzz before I saw the swarm headed my way. This was not the typical small ball of fireflies I was used to...this was a six-foot long cloud. And I could tell by the excited chatter, they were ready for a rumble!

25

"What the heck is that?" Darbie demanded.

"That's just some of my friends coming to say hello." I widened my stance. "And they aren't the only ones."

"Well, I have a few friends with me as well." Darbie let out a whistle. "We'll just see how my Venus flytrap deals with your little bugs."

While Darbie scanned the woods, GiGi lifted her hands and sent a bolt of magic at Darbie, hitting her in the chest and knocking her to the ground.

Darbie immediately jumped up. "You wanna play old witch? Let's play!"

It was like everyone materialized out of thin air. Stepping out from behind one of my Azalea bushes, Zoie, in her gargoyle form, lifted the wand from Black Forest King and sent a stream of electricity to the Venus flytrap creeping out from behind one of the trees. It struck one of his welwitschia vines, but it didn't stop his progression.

Emerging from behind the castle, dozens of woodland creatures flanked Alex and Grant—both of whom had also shifted. And opening the front door, Mom stepped outside.

"*Now* we got us a fight," GiGi cackled.

Screaming at the top of her lungs, Darbie took off at a run, magic spewing from her outstretched hands...straight for GiGi. But she didn't get far. Mom hurled a fireball at Darbie's feet, tripping her up. As Darbie rolled to a stop, GiGi hit her with a stream of energy, causing Darbie to cry out and roll on the ground.

Turning away from them, I caught sight of a tangle of kudzu rapidly ascending on Alex, Grant, and the woodland animals. Shouting for them to be aware, I smiled as the animals began to chew through the kudzu, while Alex and Grant used their razor-sharp claws to rip and shred the vines.

Not to be outdone, the fireflies danced around the Venus flytrap's mouth as Zoie and Needles both tried shredding the "leaves that cannot die" with magic and porcupine quills.

Since Mom and GiGi were focused on Darbie...and Alex, Grant, and the woodland animals were going to town on the kudzu...I turned my attention to the Venus flytrap. This was where I could help.

As Zoie sent another stream of energy to the hybrid plant, and Needles cut a chunk out of the Venus flytrap's neck with his sharp quills, I conjured up a machete and started hacking away at the base of the plant where the stem met the welwitschia leaves —metaphorically cutting it off at the knees.

The Venus flytrap was too busy trying to eat the fireflies, it barely realized the damage it was undergoing. Not until it was too late. Meeting Needles' eyes, I gave him a nod. Pulling out two new quills from his back, Needles sliced the quills through the plant's neck. Seconds later, the Venus flytrap's head rolled to the ground.

The anguished cry from Darbie made my blood run cold. Turning, I raised my hands to erect a shield as a blast of energy was hurled my way. Unfortunately, I never got a chance to put up the shield—instead, GiGi stepped in front of the blast in an effort to protect me.

The stream knocked GiGi two feet in the air before she came crashing down—landing on her hip. Crying out in pain, GiGi finally rolled to a stop. Mom threw up a protection shield around GiGi as Darbie continued to lash out at GiGi and bombard her with paralyzing pain from the magical energy blast.

I'm not sure how to explain what happened next except to say instinct took over. Knowing I had to stop Darbie at any cost, I tried to think of what Black Forest King would do.

Releasing my own angry cry, I dropped to the ground and slammed my fists against the earth. The burst of energy that radiated out of my body was so immense, it blew Mom's and Darbie's hair around them. It also caused the ground to shake and rumble, throwing Darbie off balance.

That was all the distraction Mom and I needed.

Leaping to my feet to stand by Mom, we lifted our hands and threw all the combined energy we could at Darbie. Even though she tried to counter with her own magic, she was no match for Mom and me. Within seconds, Darbie dropped her arms in defeat, and Grant leaped off the kudzu he'd been ripping apart and tackled Darbie to the ground. Shifting to human form, he engaged his binder orb and encased Darbie in the invisible shield—making it impossible for her to use magic of any kind.

Alex and Zoie shifted back to human form.

"Everyone okay?" Alex called out.

"I've been better," GiGi grumbled, staggering to her feet.

"I'll say!" Needles laughed as he flipped in the air, his wings a deep purple.

"The kudzu is dying," Zoie said. "Is that supposed to happen?"

"Yes." I sidled up next to her and a couple woodland creatures who'd been chomping through the vines and leaves. "Without Darbie's magic summoning them, they will die off."

"I'm gonna have one hell of a bruise on my hip and leg," GiGi whined.

I whirled and glared at her. "What were you thinking? Why the heck did you step in front of Darbie's stream? You *know* I can heal five times faster than you, GiGi! Have you forgotten it once only took me a day to recover from a gunshot wound to the shoulder, for pity's sake? Darbie's jolt of magic wouldn't have done near the damage to me as it did to you."

"You're my granddaughter," GiGi snapped. "I ain't gonna let nothing happen to you if I can help it."

I rolled my eyes...but then hugged her in gratitude.

"Thanks, GiGi."

"Can we please talk about that crazy thing you did, Shayla?" Zoie demanded, hands on hips. "What *was* that?"

"I'd like to know as well," Mom said, wrapping her arm around my waist. "How did you know to do that?"

I shrugged. "I didn't know. I was so angry at Darbie for hurting GiGi, I immediately thought about Dad and asked myself how he'd handle the situation. I know he expresses his anger or worry by causing the island to shake like an earthquake...and so I wondered if I could do the same, only on a smaller scale."

"Guess now you know," Zoie quipped. "It was *awesome!*"

"Black Forest King says the same thing," Needles said, drifting down to my shoulder.

"I'll say!"

"You did great, Princess!"

"Did you see the way I evaded that vine?"

132

"Did you see me almost get eaten?"

"I think we deserve nectar!"

On and on the swarm of fireflies went as they flew around my head.

"Black Forest King wants to know how everything went." Needles zipped up from my shoulder and did a somersault in the air. *"I'll go brief him on our successful attack."*

"Wait for us!"

"We want to share our part as well!"

"He'll be so proud of us!"

Needles and the fireflies flew to the back of the castle and within seconds, I lost sight of them.

"Is it okay to be sad that the Venus flytrap died?" Zoie asked. "I mean, if it hadn't been so evil, it would have been cool."

I glanced down at the Venus flytrap's head resting on the ground, mouth still open. "I can't disagree. But manipulating plants like Darbie did is not only harmful, but cruel."

"I'm going to take GiGi down to her cottage and look at her hip," Mom said. "Maybe make a magical poultice or two. Then I'm going to go see your father."

"And I'm going to call PADA and let them know about Darbie," I said. "It's still pretty early. Maybe they'll send Zane and Kara our way to pick her up."

"That would be awesome," Zoie said. "I really liked them." Zoie's eyes widened. "If they *do* send Zane and Kara tonight, maybe they can stay for dinner? I better run inside the castle and see what you have lying around in the refrigerator."

26

"I'm happy for you, Shayla." Zane wrapped an arm around my shoulder as we stood in my backyard, staring up at the stars and trees.

I clinked my wineglass against his. "Thank you. I couldn't be happier." I took a sip of my wine and glanced sideways at him, waggling my eyebrows. "You and Kara seem to be getting along pretty well."

He grinned but didn't say anything...just took a sip of his wine.

It ended up Zane and Kara both made the trip to Enchanted Island to pick up Darbie—more for visiting than anything. Zane could have done the trip solo, but Kara had not visited the island yet, so it was a chance for all of us to get together since they'd stay overnight before heading to PADA's prison in the morning. Zoie declared there were enough items in my refrigerator and pantry to make spaghetti, quick bread with garlic butter, a salad, and an apple dump cake for dessert. Grant drove back to town and picked up Serena and Aunt Starla and brought them back to the castle to help us celebrate.

While everyone else was busy, Alex and I talked, and we decided it was the perfect time to announce our wedding date. After all, what better time to make the announcement than when Zane and Kara were on the island?

"Come back inside you two," Zoie called out from a doorway in the castle. "I'm ready to serve dessert."

The apple dump cake was delicious—no surprise there. It didn't take long after that for everyone to wind down, and the party soon broke up. When everyone was gone, and Zoie was upstairs in the room that used to be mine when I was a kid—the princess tower—Alex and I started down the path that would take us to Black Forest. Midway there, we stopped to gaze out at the location that would soon become Mom's new home.

"Not too much longer now, and I'll pass Mom every time I visit Dad." I slipped my hand into Alex's. "I never thought that would happen."

"I'm happy for them...and for you. I know this is something you've always wanted."

"I've always wanted for them to be happy." I released his hand, walked over to a poplar tree, and ran my hand down its trunk. "I hated the fact my dad had to make the choice he did. I understand it —more so now than when I was a kid—but even though I under-stand why he made the choice to leave my mom and return to Black Forest...it doesn't mean I don't hurt for them. My dad is my mom's one and only love. And vice versa. Yet they cannot be together."

"It's the most epic, tragic love story ever told."

"It is," I agreed.

"Did you really think you could visit Black Forest without me?" Needles zipped by us, his wings glowing purple and green.

"It was worth a shot," Alex said, grabbing my hand and following Needles.

A few minutes later, Alex and I stopped in front of a majestic pine tree and waited for entrance inside the forest.

"Princess Shayla. And Alex Stone. It is good to see you both." The pine lifted one of its heavy branches. *"Black Forest King is excited about your visit."*

We jogged through the forest, jumped over fallen logs, and even leaped over a stream or two before finally coming to a large clearing in the woods.

"Hey, Dad." I jumped up onto one of his tall roots and ran down the length of it until I reached his trunk. "Sorry I waited so long before coming to see you, but I knew Mom wanted to see you after she took care of GiGi."

"It is okay, Daughter of my Heart. Your mother, as well as Needles and the fireflies, told me about what took place."

"Shayla, GiGi, and Serenity did a fantastic job taking down Darbie," Alex said.

"With a lot of help from me!" Needles wove his way around Dad's branches, weaving in and out of the leaves. *"I'm the one who cut off the head of the Venus flytrap, Gargoyle. Don't forget that part of the story."*

"Like any of us could," Alex joked.

Dad chuckled. *"I am just glad GiGi was not seriously hurt. Any of you for that matter."*

"We're all fine," I assured him.

"I also heard how you used your connection with the island to distract Darbie," Dad said. *"Very smart of you, Shayla."*

"I don't know how I knew to do it. I just did." I shrugged. "I just thought about how you've done it and wondered if I could do it as well."

"The bond and connection I have to the island is also in you, Daughter of my Heart. For you are a part of me."

Tears filled my eyes. "I see that now."

"Did I mention I killed the Venus flytrap?" Needles joked, breaking the mood. *"Just like I used to defeat my foes back in the day."*

"What day was that?" Alex asked.

Needles' wings turned blood red, and he zipped over to hover near Alex's face. *"Never you mind, Gargoyle. If I told you, I'd have to kill you."*

I let out a bark of laughter. "Alex and I stopped by for a reason, Dad." I plopped down and patted the ground for Alex to come sit next to me. "We've decided on a wedding date."

"That is wonderful, Shayla. What have you decided?"

"A September wedding in Black Forest—if that works for you?" I grinned. "Late September on the island is just slightly cooler than summer. Perfect for an evening wedding."

"I could not be happier for the two of you, Alex Stone. I assume you have told the others?"

"At dinner tonight," I said.

"What part am I playing in the wedding?" Needles asked, floating down to hover in front of me. *"Do I get to help Black Forest King officiate?"*

I laughed.

"No way," Alex said. "Not happening."

"You don't get a say, Gargoyle. You aren't in charge of the wedding."

"I beg to differ," Alex said.

I held up my hand to stop the argument about to unfold.

"I already have a job in mind for you, Needles." I slipped my hand into Alex's and squeezed, giving him a quick smile. "I thought maybe you could walk me down the aisle."

I didn't know it was possible for animals to tear up—but that's exactly what Needles did. *"You want* me *to walk you down the aisle, Princess? You're sure?"*

I nodded. "Yes. You and Mom. Well, more like fly me down."

Needles lifted his little head and placed a paw against his chest. *"Nothing would make me happier, Princess Shayla, daughter of the great Black Forest King."*

A tear slipped down my cheek. "Then it's settled. You and Mom will walk me down the aisle."

"What about GiGi?" Needles asked, his wings glowing silver and gold. *"She better have an important role, or she'll hex us all."*

"Truer words," Alex muttered.

"Not to worry," I said. "I have the perfect role for GiGi."

"And what is that, Shayla?" Dad mused.

I grinned. "Flower girl."

* * *

Are you ready for the next book in the series? Then click here and get *Deadly Goodbye* now. Find out what happens when a going away party for a witch turns deadly. Can Shayla, Needles, and Alex solve the case before Zoie heads to prom? All in a day's work on Enchanted Island. My Book

* * *

Love the idea of a Valkyrie witch teaming up with a Fallen Angel to solve crimes? Then the paranormal cozy series, A Kara Hilder Mystery, should be right up your alley! This crime-solving duo not only works for their supernatural town of Mystic Cove, but they also work for the Paranormal Apprehension and Detention Agency—which means they travel a lot to take down bad guys. Find out what happens when a Valkyrie with magical abilities teams up with a Fallen Angel in Book 1, *Sounds of Murder* My Book

Have you read the hilarious adventures of Ryli Sinclair and Aunt Shirley? This traditional cozy mystery series is always fast-paced and laugh-out-loud funny. But what else would you expect from Aunt Shirley—a woman who has at least two deadly weapons on her at all times and carries her tequila in a flask shoved down her shirt? Come and see what all the fuss and laughter is about with Book 1, *Picture Perfect Murder*! My Book

Love the idea of a bookstore/bar set in the picturesque wine country of Sonoma County? Then join Jaycee, Jax, Gramps, Tillie, Detective Connors, and the whole gang in this traditional cozy series as they solve murders while slinging suds and chasing bad guys in this family-oriented series. Book 1 is *Murder on the Vine!* My Book

Do you love the idea of a time-traveling, cold-case solving witch? Then Lexi and her side-kick detective familiar, Rex the Rat, are just what you're looking for! Check out their first stop to 1988 in *Time After Time.* My Book

How about a seaside mystery? My stepdaughter and I write a mystery where high school seniors pair up with their grandma and great-aunt! This series is part Nancy Drew and part Veronica Mars. Book one, *Seaside & Homicide*: My Book

Or maybe you're in the mood for a romantic comedy...heavy

on comedy and light on sweet romance? Then the Trinity Falls series is for you! You can start with Book 1, *Blazing Trouble*: My Book

Looking for a paranormal cozy series about a midlife witch looking to make a new start with a new career? Then A Witch in the Woods is the book series for you! A game warden witch, a talking/flying porcupine, and a gargoyle sheriff! Grab Book 1, *Deadly Claws* now: My Book

ABOUT THE AUTHOR

Jenna writes in the genres of cozy/paranormal cozy/ romantic comedy. Her humorous characters and stories revolve around over-the-top family members, creative murders, and there's always a positive element of the military in her stories. Jenna currently lives in Missouri with her fiancé, step-daughter, Nova Scotia duck tolling retriever dog, Brownie, and her tuxedo-cat, Whiskey. She is a former court reporter turned educator turned full-time writer. She has a Master's degree in Special Education, and an Education Specialist degree in Curriculum and Instruction. She also spent twelve years in full-time ministry.

When she's not writing, Jenna likes to attend beer and wine tastings, go antiquing, visit craft festivals, and spend time with her family and friends. Check out her website at http://www. jennastjames.com/. Don't forget to sign up for the newsletter so you can keep up with the latest releases! You can also friend request her on Facebook at jennastjamesauthor/ or catch her on Instagram at authorjennastjames.

Made in United States
North Haven, CT
31 December 2024

63789171R00085